Devour

Hellish, #2

Charity Parkerson

Without limiting the rights under copyright(s) reserved above and below, no part of this publication may be reproduced, stored in or introduced into a retrieval system, or transmitted, in any form, or by any means (electronic, mechanical, photocopying, recording, or otherwise) without the prior permission of the copyright owner.

Please Note

The scanning, uploading, and distributing of this book via the internet or via any other means without the permission of the copyright owner is illegal and punishable by law. Criminal copyright infringement, including infringement without monetary gain, is investigated by the FBI and is punishable by up to 5 years in federal prison and a fine of $250,000. Please purchase only authorized electronic editions, and do not participate in or encourage electronic piracy of copyrighted materials. Brief passages may be quoted for review purposes if credit is given to the copyright holder. Your support of the author's rights is appreciated. Any resemblances to person(s) living or dead, is completely coincidental. All items contained within this novel are products of the author's imagination.

--Warning: This book is intended for readers over the age of 18.

Introduction

The battle between Vampire and Demon rages on.

It's been two months since journalist Jonathan Jones uncovered a band of demons kidnapping women from Tortola. His run-in with the pack left him with him two choices—turn vampire or die. Now, as part of clan Hellish, Jonathan must learn a new way of life. He also has a huge problem—the turning has left him mated to the vampire prince, Niall. Unfortunately, Niall isn't who owns Jonathan's heart.

Torn between Cin, the Scottish vampire who's been his whole world for six years, and the vampire whose blood bond has Jonathan craving more, Jonathan has to find a way to hang on to his sanity. Between trying to uncover the demons' secret agenda, a kidnapped demon spawn in their garage, and a love triangle tearing apart the clan, the Hellish group has their hands full. They need to work things out before the world comes to an end— literally.

Chapter 1

The small of Jonathan's back called to him. The man had been sleeping on his stomach for hours. Niall would know. He'd been watching him. The bond between them was more than a sickness, and deeper than any addiction. He'd only turned one other human in his seven hundred years on earth. Niall hadn't been allowed to touch that man either. Jonathan was different. He was right there, within reach, and taunting Niall with an existence that didn't belong to him. Niall had gone away, hoping he wouldn't do exactly as he was doing now— craving a man only feet away he could never have.

As if the invisible link that bound them pulled him closer, Niall moved to Jonathan's side. For several long minutes, he fought himself before touching his lips to the spot that held him captivated. Jonathan didn't stir. Niall took advantage and did it again. His lips moved higher, savoring every bump in Jonathan's spine. He could've easily moved lower as well. The gods knew how badly Niall wanted to drag his tongue over the curve of Jonathan's ass. A low gasp caught in the back of Jonathan's throat. Niall heard it like the loudest of gunshots. Before he did something he wouldn't regret, Niall climbed into the empty spot next to Jonathan on the bed and stared at the man. With Jonathan's eyes closed, Niall was free to enjoy the sight of his blood mate unimpeded. The dark slash of perfect eyebrows and the curve of his cheek; those things belonged to Niall, yet they didn't.

Two months ago, Niall had turned Jonathan to save his life after a demon Niall's clan was battling had sliced the man's throat. There were a thousand problems with that act, starting with how Niall had always secretly craved Jonathan, and ending with how they were now bound for eternity. Oh, and Jonathan was in love with one of Niall's best friends. So, yeah, everything about this sucked.

For Niall, besides the blood bond, the problem was Jonathan himself. Not only was the man two steps beyond sexy with his sparkling green eyes and choppy brown hair, he was crazy-smart and deliciously perverted. Most people wouldn't know that last part. Niall wasn't most people. As the fourth son of the vampire king, Niall was too far down the line to ever ascend to the throne, especially since they were all immortal. However, his untainted royal blood— passed down from the Gods — gave him powers most vampires didn't have—like the ability to save Jonathan's life when no one else could, and to see into anyone's mind no matter how they tried shutting him out. That last part was a blessing and a curse. No one could stand against his interrogation, shut him from their dreams, or keep him from their perverse fantasies. The downside of no one keeping him out was no one kept him out. There was never a moment's peace. Never any solitude. All Niall knew was noise.

Sometimes he could focus on a solitary soul and everything would slow to a crawl—like now. Jonathan was soothing. Niall wanted to soak him in. Jonathan shifted in his sleep. His hand sought Niall's, as if searching for an anchor. As their fingers linked, Niall released a slow breath through his nose, trying to control his true nature. He was at heart a beast. Jonathan was his blood mate, and Niall was the man's prince. By law, there was nothing stopping him from rolling Jonathan beneath him and claiming the man as his. Their laws were the only thing not standing in his way.

Instead of ruining his friendship with Cin, the vampire who'd won Jonathan's heart, Niall closed his eyes and pushed his way inside Jonathan's dream. A smile touched his lips the instant Niall caught his first glimpse of Jonathan's nighttime fantasy. The man was spread eagle in the grass, staring up at a full moon. Even the man's dreams were peaceful.

"I wondered when you'd show up," Jonathan said without turning his head. It was a fair call. Niall was guilty of visiting Jonathan's dreams almost nightly. It was the safest way to soothe his desire to claim his mate without destroying anything tangible.

"You know I can't resist. Did you know most people don't have control over their dreams? But I swear you do. It's obvious you're aware you're dreaming, where most people are not, and shape your surroundings to suit your mood."

Jonathan's gaze locked on Niall at the claim. The man's smile caused Niall's stomach to cramp with want. "It isn't me I'm trying to please. You're the one who needs a break from all the noise."

Niall's chest tightened. Eternity had been especially cruel to him many times. Jonathan was no exception. The man was perfect in every way, except one—he'd never belong to Niall. He sucked it up as always.

"Does that mean I'm free to join you?" Niall asked, motioning to the spot next to Jonathan on the ground.

With a pat to grass, Jonathan lured Niall in. "Please do. I've kept your spot warm. I suppose, now that you realize I can somewhat control my dreams, you'll be putting in requests," Jonathan said as Niall settled in next to him.

Niall waited until he was on his back, shoulder to shoulder with Jonathan before responding. "Maybe I should." He hadn't meant for his voice to come out in a growl, but he couldn't stop. The idea of Jonathan giving him anything, even in a dream, was too much temptation.

A low chuckle rumbled from Jonathan. "If it's sexual, I'll need measurements. I'd hate to insult you one way or the other."

A bark of laughter escaped Niall. He snagged Jonathan's hand and brought it to his lips. For a full minute, he simply held it there while breathing in the man's scent. It was sweet—like he bathed in cotton candy. "If you'd asked, I would've asked for this. Just this. Your time is more precious than anything."

"You're sad," Jonathan said, sounding as if he'd pushed the words through a straw. Fuck. He'd forgotten to shield his thoughts from Jonathan. Normally, no one

12

could breach his mind without his permission. As with all things now, Jonathan was different. Moments before Niall had turned Jonathan, Jonathan had freely offered his blood to heal Niall from an injury. When Jonathan had been dying, Niall hadn't considered that before giving Jonathan the blood needed to pull him from death's clutches. Their reasons for the blood exchange didn't matter. It was equally unimportant no one had explained their world to Jonathan. The exchange was complete and binding for all eternity. They were now blood-mated vampires. In their world, it was the equivalent of a marriage, and it was permanent. There was no such thing as divorce—only the final death. Niall wouldn't be allowed to turn another human as long as Jonathan lived. The man's existence changed everything for Niall. That didn't mean he had to let

Jonathan feel his loneliness.

"You should kiss me and take it away," Niall said, infusing as much humor as he could drum up into his voice and only half joking. Damn, he loved when Jonathan caved and kissed him. Of course, it was only a dream. He'd never kissed Jonathan in reality.

Jonathan chuckled. "I never know if you're toying with me."

Before he could stop himself, Niall rolled and straddled Jonathan's hips, pinning him to the ground. He stared down at the man he couldn't shake. His green irises no longer held any trace of human. Now, they glowed with immorality. Niall had never wanted anyone more. "You should kiss me and take it away," he repeated.

Jonathan couldn't hide his hunger, especially from Niall. His fingers curled around the hem of Niall's T-shirt. The

14

material tightened across Niall's back as the man drew him down. Their gazes never wavered from each other. Niall's mouth watered. His palms landed on the ground on either side of Jonathan's head. He didn't stop moving until barely an inch separated them.

"Take it from me," Niall whispered, needing Jonathan's kiss.

Jonathan closed the final gap between them. When their lips met, the knot living in Niall's chest loosened. He didn't deepen their kiss. Instead, he let his lips linger, giving Jonathan all the power. Jonathan could push him away or go as far as he liked. Niall would accept either fate. At least, that was what he told himself until Jonathan's mouth opened over Niall's bottom lip. He realized then how often he told himself lies. Niall told himself he'd be okay. Jonathan was better off with his clansman, Cin. He'd let Jonathan choose his fate. As their tongues met, Niall saw all those things for the falsehoods they were. Eternity was long. Too long to fight fate. They were meant to be together.

"Niall," Jonathan whispered as he switched angles. "You're a hole missing from my heart. Don't tell, okay?" he said before reclaiming Niall's mouth. He understood. Jonathan loved Cin; so did Niall. Life had such a sick sense of humor.

"No more," Niall begged, because his heart couldn't take it. He pulled from Jonathan's dream and waited for the man to wake. With his gaze locked on Jonathan's sleeping form, he didn't realize Cin was there until his old friend spoke.

"You're back," Cin said quietly, obviously not wanting to wake Jonathan. Niall moved to leave the bed. He had no right. Cin set his hand on Niall's chest, stopping him. "No. Stay." He climbed into bed at Jonathan's other side.

"I'm sorry," Niall whispered, seeing all his fears come to life. He'd been back amongst his clan less than three hours and already he'd spent every single one of those seconds with Jonathan and stolen into Cin's bed to be closer to his blood mate. "I know I shouldn't be in here."

"You're my prince and Jonathan's mate. You have every right."

Sadness washed over him. This was why he'd stayed away. He'd known Cin would feel the weight of obligation. Niall's throat burned. For over six years, Cin and Jonathan had been in love before this...

"I should go."

Jonathan's grip tightened on Niall's hand. They were so connected at all times of the day, he'd forgotten they were holding hands. His gaze shot to Jonathan's face. One light green eye popped open. Jonathan's mouth turned up in one corner.

"Niall." He rolled back into Cin's hold, letting Niall know Jonathan was equally aware of Cin's presence.

"Hey, babe." Even Niall heard the breathless note to his voice. "Cin tells me you've been sleeping a lot—like you need my blood."

Jonathan's disappointment hit Niall like a tidal wave washing over him, making it hard for him to breathe. "You only came in here to feed me." It wasn't a question. Jonathan was sure in his knowledge Niall wanted nothing else and would disappear again the moment it was done.

This is all I'm allowed to give you. Don't steal it from me.

Jonathan chewed his bottom lip but gave Niall a short nod.

"Thank you for this," Cin said over Jonathan's shoulder.

18

Niall tore his gaze away from Jonathan's beautiful eyes and focused on Cin. "It's no problem. I worried this might happen."

"What?" Jonathan asked, pulling Niall's attention back his way.

Because he couldn't lie to this man, Niall gave him brutal honesty. "You can survive on Cin's blood alone, but you'll always feel a bit weak if you do. His blood isn't as powerful as mine, and I'm the one who turned you."

How often?

Niall understood Jonathan's mental question. He wanted to know how often he'd be forced to suffer through drinking from Niall. The draw between them was almost crippling every second of the day, but when feeding... It was only a matter of time before this blew up in their faces.

Every four to six weeks, probably closer to four.

To Niall's surprise, a smile exploded across Jonathan's face. "You can't go away again. I've got you trapped now."

"Is it still a trap if I willingly chose it?"

Jonathan's mouth quirked. "If we're getting philosophical, it'll have to wait until I'm not so tired."

At the reminder, Niall dropped Jonathan's hand and cupped the back of his head, drawing the man closer. He could offer his wrist, but Niall couldn't resist pulling Jonathan in and offering his throat instead. Jonathan held his stare. Niall moved slower than ever before, dragging out the anticipation. Teasing himself. Jonathan's mouth on his skin was a sensation he wanted to savor.

It was worse than expected. The lust

lingering from Jonathan's dream mixed with Jonathan's purposeful teasing nearly caused Niall to come in his jeans once Jonathan's mouth touched his neck. Jonathan wasn't content to take Niall's blood and send him on his way. The man treated the exchange like a test of wills. His lips brushed Niall's throat in a lingering kiss before parting. The man's tongue caressed Niall's vein. The only thing saving Niall from complete loss of control was Cin's presence, holding Niall's gaze over Jonathan's shoulder. Light blue eyes held him pinned in place as Jonathan's fangs pierced Niall's skin. Cin's cheeks flushed as if it was happening to him. He found himself reaching for Cin's hand. When their palms met, Niall's lungs finally filled with air. They were in this together.

Niall.

The longing in Jonathan's voice as it filled Niall's head was massive. He knew that whatever Jonathan asked of him in that tone, he'd get.

You have to make me stop, Niall. His short fingernails scraped Niall's side, heading for the waistband of Niall's jeans. *I don't want to stop.*

It was hell, but Niall pushed Jonathan away, allowing Cin to pull the man against his chest. The lust coating the air was cloying. Niall could scarcely breathe from it.

His fingers were still linked with Cin's. Cin tightened his grip when Niall tried pulling away. "You should stay."

With a shake of his head, Niall finally managed to free himself. "Jonathan needs you to care for him."

Cin's lips brushed Jonathan's shoulder, but his gaze never left Niall's.

"Tell him, Jonathan. He should stay."

The lust dripping from Cin's offer almost convinced Niall.

"You should stay," Jonathan said, making it even harder for Niall to pull away, especially when Jonathan's thoughts hit him. Images of the three of them together, enjoying every fantasy Niall ever experienced. Niall couldn't draw a breath around the desire. Against his better judgment, Niall dragged his thumb down Jonathan's bottom lip. His gaze locked on the sight. He wanted to capture that lip between his teeth as he sank inside his mate. Temptation was a cruel bitch.

If I thought you meant it, I'd stay.

If I thought you'd stay, I'd mean it.

"Let Cin ease the ache."

Niall slipped from the bed before he did something he couldn't take back.

Who'll ease you?

The question came as Niall closed the bedroom door behind him. He didn't let the inquiry slow him. *No one will until you do, baby.*

Since Niall couldn't shut Jonathan out, he turned his thoughts to the reluctant guest he had locked in the garage. His frustration needed some form of relief.

*

Cin's hand slid down Jonathan's torso. "He's right. I can feel the way your body aches."

"That's because you're holding me."

Jonathan meant every word; then again, he didn't. Short of tying Jonathan and Niall to the bed, he couldn't force his will on either man. Not to mention, both were immortal. They were too strong for any human binds. He could draw symbols to trap them, but not without trapping himself and pissing them off. For now, if he couldn't convince Niall to join them, he'd have to make Jonathan forget about the mate he couldn't have.

"You should use me," Cin said, luring Jonathan with his voice.

Instead of attacking Cin as Cin hoped, Jonathan rolled and met his gaze. "You should kiss me."

The green eyes he'd fallen in love with, made brighter by the flush of arousal on Jonathan's cheeks, had Cin being gentler than he wanted. He leaned in slowly, needing to savor the moment. Cin watched as Jonathan's eyes fell closed. He heard the man's heart rate increase. When their lips met, Jonathan hummed as if Cin's mouth was what he'd been waiting for his entire life. Everything else fell away. Their tongues met and retreated before entwining. Cin's heart turned over in his chest. This man was the greatest love of his life. There was nothing he wouldn't do for him.

Jonathan's fingers skimmed his side as he sought the hem of Cin's shirt. Cin leaned away so Jonathan could pull it over his head.

"This is love," Jonathan said while holding his stare.

He sounded so fierce it confused Cin. "I know."

"I'm not using you," Jonathan said, making Cin realize he'd given Jonathan the wrong impression of his intentions.

"I know," Cin repeated. "Does that mean I'm not allowed to make love to my baby?"

He felt Jonathan's muscles relax. "I'm sorry. Just ignore me. Everything is all fucked up inside my head. You're too important to me. I don't ever want you to think you're not my world."

"Oh, I know I am," Cin said, shaping Jonathan's erection through his underwear. "And I expect you to cater to my every need."

A wicked smile twisted Jonathan's lips. "Is that so?"

Cin nodded. "Right now, in fact."

While holding Cin's gaze, Jonathan reached for the zipper of Cin's jeans. "Tell me all about these needs."

After rolling out of Jonathan's reach, Cin stood beside the bed and stripped as he complied with Jonathan's request. "First, I need to feel your bare skin against mine."

With a nod, Jonathan shimmied out of his clothes. "Go on."

"Having your cock beating against the back of my throat is also a huge requirement for me."

Jonathan openly stroked his erection, teasing Cin with the sight. "I'm sure I can accommodate you."

"Can you?" Cin asked as he snagged

Jonathan's ankle and dragged him to the edge of the bed. Surprised laughter filled the room, making Cin smile at the sound. His chest filled with love and pride. This was his man. He couldn't remember a time when he wasn't owned by Jonathan. The man's laughter died away as Cin swallowed his cock. Jonathan was easily the most sexual being on the planet. His hips lifted, openly taking what he wanted from Cin. Cin only let it go on for a minute before allowing Jonathan's erection to slip from his lips so he could move lower. He sucked Jonathan's balls between his lips, savoring Jonathan's moans before moving lower. The way Jonathan pulled his hair as Cin tongued the man's asshole had Cin's dick leaking.

Saliva ran down Cin's chin. He swiped his face on Jonathan's inner thigh, wiping away some of the moisture. His fangs grew at the sound of Jonathan's blood rushing through his veins. He sank them into the vein in Jonathan's thigh. Blood filled his mouth. It was Jonathan mixed with Niall. A loud moan escaped Cin. He felt Jonathan's orgasm hit as Cin dragged the man's blood into his mouth. He sealed the wound and licked a path to Jonathan's stomach. The man's cum was Cin's reward. He swiped his tongue through the mess, letting the salty flavor mix with the copper of Jonathan's blood. Cin savored every last drop before pushing Jonathan's knees higher, positioning his cock at Jonathan's hole and sliding inside. Jonathan's body took over, pulling him deeper. He sucked in a breath as Jonathan moved beneath him, matching Cin's rhythm as he rocked inside Jonathan.

"You're so fucking gorgeous," Jonathan growled, urging Cin on. "No one is more beautiful than you are while fucking me. Your face is hard and your eyes glow while your fangs cut into your lip. I don't ever want it to end. Goddamn, the things you do to me."

Cin tilted his chin to the ceiling and pivoted his hips, trying to get deeper. He'd climb inside Jonathan and never leave if he could.

"You make my dick so hard, Cin. Let me have it. Give me your orgasm. It belongs to me."

The spring that had been winding tighter by the second inside Cin gave way. The pressure squeezing his balls burst from his dick, bowing Cin's spine and tearing a roar from his throat. As his muscles relaxed, in the aftermath of Jonathan, Cin dropped his chin and met Jonathan's gaze. Possessiveness and obsession mixed with Cin's love and desperation, creating something so ugly it was beautiful. Goddess Celeste knew he would level this whole goddamn planet just to have five minutes alone with Jonathan. May God have mercy on them all.

Chapter 2

Niall hated leaving Jonathan after feeding
him. In truth, he hated walking away from
his mate at all. It seemed as if that was all
he ever did. At first, his leaving had been
about finding the demon who'd gotten
them into this mess to begin with. Then,
the blood bond had settled in. Now
everything was about making Jonathan's
life easier. Niall had headed first to New
York and dealt with Jonathan's job. He'd
put the idea in their heads that Jonathan
had moved on to bigger and better things.
It hadn't been hard to manipulate minds
at the magazine. As an award-winning
journalist, Jonathan was their star. No
one was surprised he'd found a better job,
especially since he'd once seriously dated
the boss only to end up cheated on. That
tidbit had Niall considering dropping some
erectile dysfunction into the man's brain,

but his loss was Niall's clan's gain.

From New York, he'd switched gears, going on the hunt for their missing demon pack. He wanted the one who'd harmed his mate with something akin to madness. The beast living inside Niall demanded blood for blood. He'd known the pack would find new hunting ground after Tortola had been compromised. Niall had picked up their trail in Port Allen—a twenty-two-mile stretch of sea port along the coast of Crown Haven. After months of surveillance and searching the docks, he'd set up a new home for his clan. Now they were together again. That was how Niall had ended up here, spending half the morning staring at his mate and craving what he could never have. What he shared with Jonathan wasn't love. They hadn't spent years in each other's pockets, building a partnership. This was worse. It was a gnawing, bone-deep craving that clawed at his gut all hours of the day. That was why he needed to make someone or something hurt. Lucky him; Niall had captured a demon right before Jonathan's arrival.

"What's your name?"

The demon looked down at himself. "I believe his name was Larry." He shook his head. "Such a plain name for such a handsome man. Oh, and the things he let me do to him before I took control of his body. In my real form, no less. He's a freaky fella." He cackled as if Niall didn't intend to make him hurt.

Faolan held out a water gun to Niall. With a dip of his chin, Niall accepted. He eyed the plastic toy for a second before squirting the demon. An angry-sounding growl rent the air before transforming into a moan. Demons were a masochistic lot.

"Holy water? *Mhmm*, that's an

interesting choice for a vampire. I never realized vampires were into pain play. Obviously, I prefer whips and chains, but I can get into holy water as well."

Niall exchanged glances with Faolan before responding. "Holy water has no effect on vampires," Niall said, pointing out a detail any demon should know—unless he was a young one.

"You lie," the demon spat.

At the accusation, Niall shot himself in the arm. He flashed his wrist toward the demon, showing no damage had been done. "Seems you should've polished up on your knowledge of other species before joining the fight against the human race."

"Join. Ha! You say that as if there was a choice."

Something wasn't right. The spot where the holy water hit should've healed by now. Not only was it not healing, the damage wasn't anywhere near as bad as it should be. This was no demon, but he was young—a demon spawn, perhaps.

"What's your name?" Niall asked again. "This time, don't lie. I'm much older than you. Older than you can fathom. I know this is no demonic possession. This is your true form."

Panic crossed the creature's face before sliding behind a mask of indifference. He shrugged. "I'd rather settle in for some torture. Don't let my age fool you. Names have power. Power means control. I've been controlled my whole life. You can't be any worse."

"If you won't give us your name. Tell us about the piers," Faolan demanded. "We know you're using them to kidnap women. Where are you taking them? Which dock are you using?"

The demon spawn snorted. "Ask better questions."

Niall bit back a growl. Sometimes demons could be quite literal. If they didn't ask the right questions, he'd never answer or tell plausible lies that would keep them chasing their tails for eternity. A wave of sadness washed over Niall. It wasn't his. Everything around him disappeared as he focused on Jonathan.

What's wrong?

Just feeling useless and out of place today. Get back to work. Don't worry over me.

Niall ignored Jonathan's demand. Instead, he focused harder on Jonathan, opening all his senses and climbing inside the man's head. He needed to know if Jonathan was telling him the whole truth. Jonathan was trying to push him out. All Niall felt was unnatural warmth.

Where are you?

Shower.

Niall shot to his feet. *Stay put.* He handed the water gun to Faolan. "He's yours. I have business."

Faolan dipped his chin. A smirk touched his lips. "Thank you. You know how much I love inflicting harm."

He did, but that was not why Niall was walking away. Jonathan needed him. The demon spawn wasn't going anywhere.

*

Stay put? What the hell was that supposed to mean? Jonathan ducked his head beneath the deluge of water, hoping to drown his thoughts from Niall. The air stirred at his back. Jonathan didn't lift his head. He knew Niall was there without having to look. His dick stirred. Niall was too close while Jonathan was too naked. He knew he needed to react, but he didn't know how. Cool lips touched Jonathan's nape. Jonathan's lips parted on a breath. With his mind carefully blank, Jonathan turned.

"Talk to me," Niall said, sounding heartbreakingly sweet.

"I'm taking a shower."

Niall dipped his chin. "I'm aware. It's pissing down on my good boots."

Jonathan dropped his gaze to Niall's feet. Sure enough, the man wore unlaced work boots. Jonathan's gaze traveled up Niall's body. His legs were encased in ragged jeans. A half-tucked T-shirt plastered to the man's ripped stomach as beads of water splashed from Jonathan's body onto Niall's skin. He also wore a red unbuttoned flannel shirt as if it wasn't ninety degrees outside. His outfit, combined with the full beard covering his chin, brought a certain image to Jonathan's mind.

Despite their circumstances, a snort

escaped Jonathan. "You look like a large Scottish lumberjack today."

Niall's eyes never wavered from Jonathan's face. His mouth lifted in one corner in a small smile. It was enough to bring out the man's dimples and make Jonathan's heart turn over in his chest.

"What's wrong?" Cin asked, ripping open the shower door and looking panicked.

Niall glanced over, obviously unconcerned over their current location. "That's what I'm trying to find out."

"I'm taking a shower," Jonathan repeated through numb lips.

Niall sighed long and loud. "Hand us a towel, Cin."

Cin dutifully passed one over.

Before Jonathan could protest, Niall's arms encircled him. He wrapped the towel around Jonathan's waist. His gaze held Jonathan's the entire time, as if making a point of not eyeing Jonathan's nude body. Jonathan burned every place they touched. He was hyper-aware of the way Niall carefully avoided brushing Jonathan's erection. He could've easily done so, even by accident. It wouldn't have been difficult, considering Jonathan's dick was twitching and trying to get closer to Niall.

Niall's gaze turned heated. In the man's eyes, Jonathan saw all the ways Niall would take him if they were alone. He couldn't tear his gaze away.

"There," Niall said, tucking one corner of the towel in tight and ensuring Jonathan wouldn't lose it. "Now you're sufficiently covered. You can stop thinking about how Cin will be mad at you over this and tell us what's wrong."

"Why would I be mad?" Cin asked, sounding hurt.

"I don't like being useless," Jonathan

said over the top of him before they had time to discuss things none of them wanted to talk about. This was an easier topic. "For the past couple of months, I've gone from sitting around because I was healing to sitting around because I'm useless here. I'm used to working and helping. Eternity is going to be ridiculously long if I'm forced to spend it doing nothing."

Niall nodded. His expression never changed. "All you needed to say was you were ready to work. I've got plenty for you to do. Finish your shower and then you can get started." Without another word, Niall stepped from the shower and headed for the door.

"Hold up, Niall. We need to talk," Cin called at the man's back. Niall didn't stop. If anything, he picked up the pace.

Cin growled. It sounded ridiculously sexy. "Fuck." He spun and covered

Jonathan's mouth in a hard and quick kiss. His eyes said everything his lips didn't. Cin loved him. "I can't believe you thought I'd be angry." He released a loud sigh as if exhausted by it all. "Finish your shower."

Jonathan's shoulders fell once he was alone. He was failing everyone.

*

Cin's rage boiled as he followed Niall's trail of water to the man's bedroom. Without bothering to knock, he threw open the door and stormed inside. Niall stood shirtless, looking less than surprised to see Cin.

"We have to talk about this, Niall."

"There's nothing to discuss. I'm trying my arse off here, Cin. Just leave it at that."

"I know you're trying."

"Do you?" Niall shot back. "You think talking this out will change anything? It won't. No matter which way I go, I'll lose.

I'm losing my mate already. If I claim him, I'll lose you. Tell me how talking it out will fix anything? Fuck. This is why I stayed away."

"You stayed away because you're a coward," Cin said, losing his temper. "We were right where you left us, waiting—"

Cin found his back shoved against the wall and a pissed-off Niall hovering over him before he realized it would happen. Niall's fangs were bared as if he intended to take Cin apart.

"Is this the reaction you sought? Do you need to see and feel my fury?" He leaned in, pinning Cin to the wall with his weight before loudly inhaling Cin's scent. "You smell like him. It's my mate's blood pumping through your veins." His lips touched Cin's pulse point. Cin didn't dare take a breath. He'd never seen Niall like this before. He'd always been intense, but this was different. Cin wondered if the man would kill him. After all, he was the only thing standing between Niall and Jonathan. "I can't decide if I want to drain your blood to get all of his, or kiss you so I can taste him on your lips. Is that what you hoped to hear?"

"Do it," Cin taunted, because anything, anything at all was better than living in constant suspense, waiting for the ax to fall.

Niall slammed his fist into the wall beside Cin's head. Cin refused to show an ounce of weakness. The way Niall's nostrils flared proved his temper hadn't eased upon impact. "You've been feeding him while I was away."

"Yes."

With each breath, Niall's shoulders rose and fell. "Thank you for taking care of him. You need to feed too."

"I'm fine," Cin lied. He couldn't imagine biting anyone else. Faolan had been keeping him fed so he wouldn't have to sully his teeth with a stranger. It was crazy, he knew, but fuck. He'd never have as much to offer Jonathan as Niall did. His blood would never be royal. The least he could do was keep his fangs within the clan.

Niall bared his throat. "Take my blood."

Cin stared at Niall's neck and listened to the blood pumping through his veins. Like Niall, Jonathan was a sickness. Niall shared Jonathan's blood. It was as if they were all one and the same now. It would be just like tasting Jonathan. He moved closer without realizing it. His lips touched Niall's skin. It was as if an invisible line lured him in. Cin's fangs grew. Blood filled his mouth as they pierced Niall's vein. A moan rose in his throat with no chance of him calling it back. As a royal, Niall's flavor was unique. He was rich, like the most expensive wine. Cin had to force himself not to take too much since Niall had just fed Jonathan.

As he pulled away, other hungers made themselves known. Niall was standing too close. Waves of lust rolled off his skin. They were connected through Jonathan in a way they shouldn't be, but there it was. The way Niall watched him, as if he could offer Cin endless pleasure, had Cin ready to do anything. The lines were blurred. This was Jonathan's mate. Even with desire swimming in Niall's gaze, his fury hadn't eased. Cin couldn't take the uncertainty of his life any longer. He couldn't stand the gap between them.

"Do it," Cin taunted again, recognizing

Niall was on the edge of exploding with anger.

Niall leaned closer. Barely an inch separated their mouths from touching. Cin could feel the man's every exhaled breath brushing his lips. Niall's flavor wasn't unfamiliar to him. They'd lived together hundreds of years. It was inevitable they'd give in to passion occasionally. He could already taste Niall coating his tongue. The rage in Niall's gaze dimmed. He pushed away.

"You're not him."

He snagged a box from his dresser and pushed it into Cin's arms. The man's dark expression made it that much harder for Cin to catch his breath. "Give that to Jonathan. In Tortola, things got so hectic, his laptop and all his work got left behind at the hotel. I grabbed it for him. Let him know I need him to keep doing everything he did before the turn, except now he does it for me and not a magazine. He's always been one step ahead of us. I don't expect that'll change."

"Niall," Cin said, still trying his damnedest to salvage things.

Niall ignored him. "I'll pay him whatever. Hell, royalty should have some perks, right? Also, let him know I'll back pay him for the past six years he's been working with us without knowing it."

Niall undressed and found dry clothes while giving his speech. The longer he talked, the more Cin's heart sank. Niall had made up his mind. This was how things would be between them now.

Cin cleared his throat past the lump growing there. "Seems to me, you've already decided to give up both of us." He cleared his throat again. "I would've followed you anywhere, my prince," Cin said, giving a short bow and walking away.

He no longer cared to hear what else Niall had to say. The deep hurt in Niall's eyes made Cin feel like the worst of traitors. It was funny how something could be no one's fault, yet still feel like it was everyone's.

He heard Jonathan's laughter before reaching the living room. There was a reason Faolan's name sounded like "fool-on." He always acted like an idiot and was always on. It seemed today was no different. Instead of racing into the room, hoping to see Jonathan's smile, Cin slowed his step. He worried if he burst into the room, he'd have to watch the smile slip from Jonathan's face. The man rarely smiled anymore. Instead, Cin lingered outside the door and eavesdropped.

Jonathan's voice drifted out. "Why do I get the feeling you were the court jester in your day? Wait. Was that even a thing back then?"

"Our days could get verra boring. That is, when we weren't working to survive. Back then, every day was a chore. You woke up and then worked your arse off just to make it through another day. Hauling in water, feeding animals, hunting, and doing a million things people take for granted today with a push of a button. But still, at mealtimes or at night before bed, there was no TV, or much of anything for entertainment. So, I guess I have always been a bit of a jokester. Someone had to break the monotony."

"I'm sure your efforts were appreciated."

A loud guffaw sounded throughout the room. Cin smiled. He could practically see Faol holding his stomach in laughter. "Not at all. If anything, I was a bit of a nuisance. Not that I cared, mind you. I like to make people laugh, and whether they admit to it or not, people need a reason to smile. Nowadays, I don't have as much of an audience, but I still try. It's nice to have a fresh face to entertain."

"So I'm your project now?"

Faol's voice turned serious. "Aye, if you'd like to call it that. You're sad, and I don't know how else to fix it."

Silence fell between them for long enough to make Cin feel a bit stupid for still lingering outside the door. When Jonathan spoke again, Cin's heart squeezed in his chest.

"They should've let me die. All of this could've been avoided."

"Aye, they should've," Faol said, making Cin want to rush into the room and flatten his nose. The man's next words kept his feet glued to the floor. "Then again, mayhap if Cin had turned you years ago, as he should've done, all this could've been avoided. It matters not why things are as they are. The Gods have set you on this path. Eventually, you'll find out why. Until then, keep in mind you have no control over fate, and get on with your life."

Jonathan sighed. "For future reference, don't worry too much over my mood. It's all over the place since my turning. I'm like a crazy hormonal teenager. There's no sense in you worrying about something even I can't control."

"It'll get better. Everything's just heightened—"

Since they'd moved past the heavy stuff, Cin chose to make his presence known, cutting off Faol. "I come bearing gifts."

Rather than Jonathan's smile melting

away, as Cin feared, it grew at the sight of Cin. "Hey, sexy. I'm in dire need of gifts, and you, of course," Jonathan added with a wink. Cin crossed the room and set the box on the table in front of Jonathan. He leaned forward and eyed its contents. "Wow. It's stuff that already belongs to me," Jonathan said with laughter lacing each word. Cin swept in and captured Jonathan's lips, forcing the man back against the couch until he could straddle his hips. "Mmm," Jonathan hummed against his lips. "It's even more stuff that already belongs to me."

"I think I hear someone calling my name," Faol said, laughing. "Like at the other end of the house. Possibly it came from the pub down the street," he added, his voice getting farther away.

Cin waved over his shoulder, sending the other man on his way. "Goddamn,

Jonathan. I don't want to do anything anymore but touch you. It's like I need to make up for all the many times we've been apart. I know we have forever, but damn," he said, humming the last word against Jonathan's throat. "There used to be this ice cream parlor in London. I swear, you smell just like that place. It makes me want to lick you all day." Cin could smell Jonathan's lust, hear the way his heart rate kicked up, and practically taste the endorphins in the air. "I love you," Cin said, whispering the words like a shared secret.

Jonathan massaged Cin's ass between his hands, drawing him closer and obviously not unwilling to forgo another night of working. "I love you too, baby."

"The lovey-dovey shit is boring. Get to the dick sucking already."

Cin's head whipped around in Faol's

direction. "What the hell? I thought you'd left."

Faol's wicked smile held no repentance. "I'm verra good at throwing my voice, making it seem like I'm getting farther away." He pitched his voice lower with every word, demonstrating the effect. "Now, let's see some skin."

Jonathan's body shook with laughter. That was the only reason Cin wasn't losing his shit. Jonathan patted his ass. "Tell me why you've brought my computer."

Cin reluctantly climbed from Jonathan's lap. As much as he wanted to be alone with Jonathan, he knew a lost cause when he saw one. "You're working for Niall now."

"Just Niall?"

Cin glanced over, confused by Jonathan's odd tone. "Yes. We all work for

Niall. Now you do too. So," he said, snagging the laptop from the box, "he needs your brand of research. While we're certain the demons are using this town for the same purposes as Tortola, we've yet to locate the pack. You found them without trying in Tortola. We need you to do it again."

Jonathan eyed the laptop. "That's probably long past being dead."

Cin passed the device Jonathan's way. "Find an outlet and get started. We need you."

Chapter 3

One month later...

They didn't need him. Maybe Cin had claimed Jonathan would be of use now. During the past month of research, he'd learned one thing if he'd learned nothing else—he was useless to this clan. Occasionally, he'd find a tidbit—a place they could search. The men would be off, scouting the area or doing surveillance. Jonathan was here, trapped in the house, and still marveling over the fact he couldn't find anything to eat he liked anymore.

He eyed his peanut butter and jelly sandwich with suspicion. Faolan slowed on his way to the sink. His eyebrows rose in silent question.

Jonathan spoke around the peanut butter sticking to the roof of his mouth.

"Why is this the nastiest thing I've ever had in my mouth?"

After grabbing a beer from the fridge, Faolan pulled a chair away from the table with his foot. He plopped down, facing Jonathan. "That's a good question. Why is that the nastiest thing you've had in your mouth?" he asked, twisting the cap off his bottle. He tossed the cap away before taking a long swig. "I mean," Faolan continued, "you date real men. Like, sweating, battling, burping, and farting real mean. So, how is it that a PB and J is the most disgusting thing you've ever put in your mouth? You should be able to name at least fifteen disgusting things you've had coating your tongue other than that sandwich by now."

Jonathan's shoulders shook. He tried not to choke.

Faolan wasn't finished. He plucked the sandwich from Jonathan's hands. "Let's

59

look at this logically." He took a huge bite. Faolan pulled a face before reaching for the trashcan, tossing the sandwich in and spitting out the bite. "Ugh. I can't get it off my tongue. I take it back. You've had eight, maybe nine worse things in your mouth before." Jonathan laughed harder as Faolan chugged his beer, trying to get the taste out of his mouth.

"That was my lunch slash breakfast, possibly mid-morning snack."

Faolan used Jonathan's napkin to scrape his tongue. "That wasn't food. That was diabetes. Your taste buds have changed with the turning. You need something better. Are you ready for this? Now just hear me out. You need something big and salty."

Niall's hands landed on Jonathan's shoulders and squeezed. At the contact, every nerve ending sang. Jonathan couldn't stop smiling.

"What are you two up to?"

"Faolan's trying to get me to suck his dick," Jonathan said without an ounce of shame.

"A big pretzel. I'm trying to get him to eat one of those big pretzels we have in the freezer. All it takes is a few seconds in the microwave."

Jonathan snorted.

"Then, once he's got something in his stomach, he can suck my dick if he so chooses."

Niall's low chuckle had Jonathan shaking with laughter. He massaged Jonathan's shoulders once more. Jonathan's spine relaxed against the chair as he sank into the sensation. "In all honesty, you probably do need something salty. Not Faolan's dick, of course, as I'm sure he'd like to keep it." Faolan winced. Niall ignored him. "You've changed on a biological level. Your body has different

61

needs." His body had needs, so many needs with Niall touching him. Niall turned away and headed for the freezer. "Come here."

Jonathan immediately stood and followed on Niall's heels to the freezer.

"You like sweets, correct?"

Jonathan nodded. "But they don't taste the same." He pulled a face. "It really sucks."

Niall nodded. Jonathan could feel his understanding. "You don't have to give it up. Just change the way you look at it." He pulled a container of vanilla ice cream from the freezer. Jonathon watched as he found a shaker of sea salt and some dark chocolate crumbles. After making a pile of salt and crumbles, he dipped a spoonful of ice cream in the mixture. "Try this," Niall said, holding out the spoon. Jonathan dutifully opened his mouth and accepted the bite. An explosion of salt, bitter, and sweet coated his taste buds. Jonathan's eyes fell closed as he swallowed the delicious concoction.

"Oh my God. That's amazing." His eyes opened. Jonathan stopped breathing as his gaze collided with Niall's. Hunger stared back at him, but there was something else too. Jonathan skimmed Niall's mind without thought. A wave of sadness washed over Jonathan. "I'm sorry too."

You have nothing to be sorry about.

I stole your life.

To Jonathan's surprise, Niall smiled. "No, you didn't. You gave me a reason to keep going."

"No fair," Faolan said, reminding them of his presence. "No one else can read Niall's mind unless he lets us. He's powerful. Is it because Jonathan was a Seer before the turn? Or do you think it's because he's mated to a prince?"

Horror crawled over Jonathan's skin. "Prince?"

Niall's gaze skirted away. He set the spoon on the counter.

"Oh, fook," Faolan said, coming to his feet. "I'm out."

Jonathan ignored Faolan's hasty exit. "You're a prince?"

"I assumed you knew by now."

Without thought, Jonathan growled. "How would I know? No one tells me anything. I'm just sitting around, waiting on the passing of eternity, I suppose."

Niall met his gaze. "In our world, each species has its rulers. We don't answer to the laws of man. Someone has to keep order."

Jonathan tried hard not to panic. He hated not knowing what he'd stepped into. "So I'm mated to a prince. What does that mean for me?" Even Jonathan couldn't believe how calm he sounded. There was no way Niall didn't realize Jonathan was freaking the fuck out inside.

A dimple appeared in Niall's cheek. He picked up the spoon and repeated his earlier process. Jonathan dutifully opened his mouth as Niall fed him. Niall waited until Jonathan's mouth was full before responding. "If I ever ascend to the throne, you'll rule beside me." Before Jonathan had time to panic, Niall eased his worries. "But I'm fourth in line. Considering we're all immortal, the odds of me ever ruling anything other than this merry lot of filthy clansmen are astronomical. Plus, my father would probably come back and hold the throne as a ghost to keep me from having it. No one expects anything from you, Jonathan." He continued to feed Jonathan while giving his speech. "You're here because everyone wants you here. I don't know why you can shove your way into my thoughts when no one else has ever been able to do so in the past." His smile turned sad. "Just be careful in there. It's a dark place."

Jonathan searched Niall's face. Now that he'd been told to be careful, he couldn't stop trying to read Niall's every thought. "You've gone too long without taking blood."

"I can go much longer than a regular vampire," Niall said, trying to spoon more ice cream into Jonathan's mouth.

He pushed the spoon away. "How long?"

Niall seemed to think it over. "Probably six months," he said after a minute. He nodded as if satisfied with that answer. "Six months."

"How long has it been?"

One of Niall's massive shoulders lifted in a half shrug. "Since the last time you offered me your vein."

It took all of Jonathan's willpower not

to let his mouth hang open. "Seriously? Why?"

Obviously realizing Jonathan didn't intend to let him continue with the ice cream, Niall set the spoon aside. "You've been recovering, and it's very... difficult," Niall said, as if searching for the right word, "to accept taking blood from anyone other than your mate." Niall's expression turned dark and hot. Jonathan's mouth went dry. "Basically, I have no desire to sink my fangs into anyone else."

"I'm better now. You should feed."

Niall shook his head. "I'm okay."

"You're not," Jonathan argued. "Look," he said, tempering his voice. "We can make this not so awkward. Let's do it right here, standing up with any witnesses who choose to stroll into the kitchen."

"You think I wouldn't take you in front of witnesses?" Niall asked, sounding two steps shy of deadly. "Do you really believe—given the chance—I wouldn't bend you over this sink and fook you with the whole world watching?"

If Jonathan had ever been harder in his life, he couldn't remember it. His voice turned husky with his arousal. "We can do this. Drink from my wrist. I'll keep you out of my head. Nice and impersonal."

"No one can keep me out."

"What am I thinking right now?" Jonathan shot back as quickly.

Niall focused on Jonathan. Jonathan split his attention between holding a wall between them and picturing the way Niall's lips always clung to his in dreams. He needed his thoughts to be sexual to test his wall because he knew without a doubt his thoughts would be ten times as bad once Niall touched him.

Niall's expression went from fierce to confused. "Are you keeping your mind blank?"

Jonathan felt his smile grow into something wicked. "Nope."

Without warning, Niall grabbed Jonathan's wrist and bit down. A gasp tore from Jonathan's lips at the unexpected move. He could feel Niall probing at his thoughts. It was like a feather tickling his brain. While gritting his back teeth, Jonathan did his damnedest to keep the man out. He'd been wrong. So very wrong. Jonathan had honestly believed the wrist would be a better choice. Now he couldn't stop picturing Niall's lips sucking his wrist while Jonathan's lips were wrapped around Niall's dick. A line appeared between Niall's eyes. Jonathan's heart rate kicked up and his breathing increased as he tried fighting his body's reaction. He needed to keep Niall out or the man would never agree to this again. Jonathan couldn't let him starve.

Niall licked the wound closed and tore

his mouth away. Before Jonathan could catch his breath and argue that Niall hadn't taken enough to sustain him, Niall tugged him into his arms.

"I don't like the silence. Let me in," he begged before sinking his fangs into Jonathan's throat.

A moan escaped him before Jonathan could call it back. His walls fell and every fantasy he had of being on his knees filled his head. In his mind, there was no part of Niall left unlicked. Niall pulled his hair in real life the way he did in Jonathan's fantasies. He had no clue what kept him from coming in his jeans that second. He was panting and moving against Niall's body, seeking relief from the fire threatening to burn him alive. Niall's tongue swiped Jonathan's throat. Jonathan's knees turned to mush. Only Niall's massive arms wrapped around his waist kept Jonathan from hitting the floor.

"Was it impersonal, Jonathan?" Niall's voice held a thick brogue he'd never heard the man use before as he spoke against the shell of Jonathan's ear. Without giving Jonathan time to answer, he dissipated.

Jonathan blinked. His skin chilled, leaving him feeling lost. He balled his hands into fists, trying to control the shaking. A low whistle filled the air, bringing Jonathan's head around to the door. Dougal stood with his shoulder leaned into the frame. The blond beauty of the bunch, as Jonathan had come to think of him, looked sexy as sin with the flush of arousal riding high on his cheeks.

"Dear goddess. That was the hottest thing I've ever seen." Dougal adjusted the front of his jeans, lending truth to his words.

To hide his blush, Jonathan turned his back on the man and knocked the spoon into the sink. With Niall no longer there, clouding his thoughts, the guilt set in. It could've easily been Cin witnessing him humping Niall in his clothes.

"You should go after him before he does something stupid."

Jonathan's insides twisted into knots at Dougal's words. "It's not my place."

Dougal snorted. "You have a ridiculous cut and dry outlook on life. Niall always goes to work on his sword creations when he's upset. You should go too."

A bitter smile twisted Jonathan's lips. "He doesn't want me coming after him."

"I'm sure that's not true. Nothing will ever get worked out if you don't talk to each other about it."

"I can hear his thoughts. He's begging me to leave him alone." Jonathan swallowed past the pain and bitterness of the confession. "The least I can do is honor his wishes." Because he couldn't deal with life anymore today, Jonathan pushed past

Dougal and headed for the bedroom. He would go back to bed. It wasn't like anyone needed him for anything anymore anyhow. No one would miss him.

*

"Where is everyone?" Cin asked as he washed the demon blood from his hands. He'd been interrogating the spawn for close to eight hours. Now angry-looking burn marks were left behind from the demon's acidic blood. The water turned red as it carried away the mixture down the drain. The wounds healed before Cin could dry his hands.

Faolan looked up from his book at the question. "Dougal left for town earlier. Niall is sulking with his knives and Jonathan went back to bed about an hour ago."

Worry had Cin's eyebrows drawing together. "Is he okay?"

73

Faolan shrugged. "Dougal says Jonathan gave Niall blood earlier. Maybe it's still too soon for him to be offering his vein? It's been a long time since I've been around a new turn, so I don't recall how long it takes for them to be one hundred percent."

Cin took a deep breath, calming himself. This wasn't about the turn. Jonathan had been healed from that since Niall had been giving him blood on the regular. This was depression, and Cin didn't know what to do. He didn't realize he'd spoken the confession aloud until Faolan gave his two cents on the matter.

"You should make him talk to Niall. If he won't, you should send him in to interrogate the spawn. Hell, he can't do any worse than we have. Our methods are getting us nowhere."

He was right. For a month now, they'd

taken turns torturing the young demon to no avail. The spawn may've been young in years, but he was as solid and unbending as an elder demon. Still, Cin didn't want to expose Jonathan to this side of their life.

"Jonathan is a genius. He's not cut out for the ugliness we face."

Faolan snorted. "In case you haven't noticed, that boy is stronger than we are. I'm not sure if it's the Seer blood in his veins or what, but he's freaky advanced for a new turn."

Cin couldn't deny Faolan's claim. "I'll think about it."

He started down the hall. Faolan called after him. "You'd better think quick, because shit's falling apart around here."

Since he couldn't deny it, Cin chose to ignore Faolan and concentrate on Jonathan instead. He opened their bedroom door slowly, hoping not to wake Jonathan. With their window blacked out to keep out the sun, a silent darkness met him. Cin's eyes adjusted to the dark. His senses took over, making every detail of the room stand out as if the sun shone brightly inside the room. A pillow covered Jonathan's head. He was on his stomach. Even after probing at his thoughts, Cin couldn't tell if Jonathan was asleep or tuning out the world.

He set one knee on the bed and paused. Jonathan didn't budge. Cin crawled higher up the mattress while straddling the man's ass. After bracing himself on his palms, Cin leaned in and touched his lips to the back of Jonathan's neck. A pant so low it would've been undetectable to a human's ears escaped Jonathan. Since the man wore nothing more than boxer briefs and Cin needed skin on skin, he pulled his shirt over his head, tossing it aside before going back for more.

As he looked on, Jonathan grasped at the sheets. Cin traced the bumps of Jonathan's spine with his tongue. "Cin."

Cin nearly broke at the sound of his name leaving Jonathan's lips in such a ragged whisper. He wrapped his fingers around the waistband of Jonathan's underwear and dragged them down the man's hips. The instant the bare flesh of Jonathan's sexy ass was exposed, Cin sank his teeth into the man's ass cheek. Cin's eyes fell closed. In almost seven hundred years, Cin had never found another man who kept him ensnared the way Jonathan did. The man was an itch, living under his skin.

"Damn, I've missed you today," Cin said, hearing the desperation in his voice.

"You are the love of my life. My vice."

At his confession, Jonathan rolled. He gripped the back of Cin's neck and hauled him forward. Their mouths clashed. There was no better taste in the world than Jonathan.

"I've been waiting for this."

Jonathan's confession broke something inside Cin. It fed the obsession living inside him. "I need to be inside you." Once the admission was out there, Jonathan tore at Cin's jeans, as if he felt the same desperation to be with Cin. The instant they were nude, Cin licked his fingers and stretched Jonathan's hole. Jonathan writhed beneath him. His impatience caused him to be rougher than he intended. After guiding his cock to Jonathan's asshole, the man's body took over, pulling him inside. Tight heat squeezed him, making him wonder how long he could hang on. The noises coming from the back of Jonathan's throat drove Cin insane. He kissed every place he could reach while speaking against Jonathan's skin.

"Do you remember our first night together?"

Jonathan sucked in a hiss. "Oh God."

Cin took that as a yes. "You handcuffed me to the bed. I thought I could play along. Let you continue thinking I was human and you could control me. For as long as I live, I'll never forget your face when those handcuffs shattered. You weren't afraid." Pressure climbed from his toes, beating at his crown and making his spine itch as he remembered how out of control he'd been that night. He'd never shown his true nature to a human before Jonathan. Jonathan hadn't reacted the way any other human would. Instead of screaming or running for his life, Jonathan's lust had heightened. The man beneath Cin was a sexual deviant. It was enough to blow any man's mind. "Don't be afraid now. Let me inside your head. Show me all your darkest fantasies. I can make them real."

Rather than giving in, Jonathan surged upward and flipped until he straddled Cin's hips, taking what he wanted. He rode Cin hard, stealing all Cin's thoughts. His kisses turned biting. Jonathan's fangs were bared. The sexy sight made it hard for Cin to breathe.

Jonathan's lips moved to the shell of Cin's ear. "I love you, sexy. More than words," he swore before sinking his fangs into Cin's neck. Lights exploded behind Cin's eyes—like a strobe light. Every muscle tensed to the point of tearing something before an orgasm shook him to his core. Hot semen coated his stomach and chest, letting him know he'd somehow pleased Jonathan while the man had him completely entranced. Jonathan stole his blood and seed while filling Cin's mind with images of all the dirty ways he'd allow Cin to control him. The waves of pleasure didn't relent, releasing him from their grip, until Jonathan licked the puncture wounds closed.

"Loving you is the scariest and bravest thing I've ever done," Jonathan whispered against his ear. "I gave my life away for you. Stay for a little while. I'll show you all the dark places you want to see. I've got nothing left to fear, except an eternity without you."

Cin's stomach clenched at the idea. He wanted to punish Jonathan for as much as thinking it. Cin had an hour or two he could spend teaching Jonathan a lesson. He wouldn't let a second go to waste.

Chapter 4

Cin was gone. A huge part of Jonathan recognized he should've seen that one coming. After all, Cin was always gone lately. Still, when he'd opened his eyes after hours of rough lovemaking, the empty space where Cin should have been felt like a void inside him rather than beside him. Instead of flying into a rage, Jonathan took a shower as if nothing happened. He kept his mind carefully blank. Nothing good could come of him turning things over in his head. He'd always believed, once he was like Cin, there'd be nothing left standing between them. Now, there were so many things driving them apart, he couldn't even see Cin any longer. Jonathan stared out the kitchen window, wondering how long it would take for him to snap, and what would happen when he did.

"Did Cin talk to you about helping with the interrogation of our guest in the garage?"

"There's a guest in the garage?" Jonathan asked around a bite of ice cream. He'd been attempting Niall's concoction again when Dougal had snuck up on him. Jonathan had assumed everyone was gone since he hadn't been able to find anyone when he'd rolled out of bed.

Dougal scrubbed his hands over his face before meeting Jonathan's gaze once more. He looked resigned. "I'll take that as a no. Faolan said Cin would talk it over with you."

The way Dougal's lips flattened into a line fascinated Jonathan. Still, he had Jonathan's curiosity piqued. The man had definitely said something about helping. Since Jonathan had never been more bored in his life, he wanted to know more.

"What do you need me to do?"

"Niall captured a demon spawn shortly before our arrival," Dougal said fast, as if he expected Jonathan might be angry over the news. It was ridiculous, of course. That was what the clan did—they fought evil. When Jonathan didn't react, Dougal continued, "We've been taking turns interrogating the spawn about his pack without luck. I thought you might like a stab at it."

"What's a spawn?" Jonathan asked, hoping to buy time. He knew nothing about trying to get information from a demon.

"It's the child of a demon and human."

"Oh."

Some of his panic must have shown on his face because Dougal gave his shoulder a pat. "Don't worry. He can't hurt you. We've got him trapped by ancient symbols. You'll be perfectly safe. Just have a chat with him and see if you can glean anything from his words. It's my hope, with your investigative skills, you might see something we don't."

Jonathan threw his spoon in the sink. "What the hell. Why not?"

He followed Dougal's directions to the small room built inside the garage. His steps slowed as he approached the door. It wasn't as if Jonathan hadn't seen a demon before. After all, one had killed him. Still, he didn't know what to expect. Surely a demon, even a spawn, would be furious after a month's imprisonment. Would it even look human any longer? Did spawns ever look anything other than human? Jonathan felt woefully unprepared for this task. Since he didn't have anything better to do with his time and the journalist side of him was beyond intrigued, Jonathan turned the knob and stepped inside.

The man inside sat in an

uncomfortable-looking chair. If Jonathan wasn't mistaken, the hardback wooden piece came from their kitchen table. Those always hurt his ass and back after only a few minutes. This dude had been sitting there for over a month. Although Jonathan hadn't known what to expect, he still couldn't have guessed what he'd find. This demon was gorgeous. If he thought about it, Jonathan recognized he shouldn't have been surprised. People made deals with demons. He had to think most people wouldn't do that with a red beast with horns. This man was brown-haired and brown-eyed, which might sound drab if someone had described the spawn to Jonathan. This guy was anything but. His hair hung over one eye. Even a mess couldn't dim this dude. A chiseled jaw and cut body coupled with ancient-looking tattoos and pierced nipples. Jonathan wanted to cry foul because no one had warned him the man would be shirtless.

His gaze followed Jonathan as he crossed the room. Supple lips lifted in one corner, tempting Jonathan to sigh. Jonathan couldn't help but wonder how many people had willingly traded their souls to this man simply because they hadn't heard a word he said. They'd been too mesmerized by him.

"You're new."

Jonathan rolled his shoulders as a British accent fell from the demon's tongue. Seriously, Dougal should've warned him. "Not really," Jonathan said, trying to keep his tone flat.

"Actually, I meant quite literally. You're a new turn. I'd say no more than six months. If that."

Tearing his gaze away, Jonathan spent a moment eyeing the symbols drawn on the walls and ceiling. He didn't want to admit the demon was right. Instead, he chose a different topic.

"What's your name?"

The dude smiled. It screamed wickedness. "As I've told your friends, names are power. I have no intention of handing over such control."

Jonathan claimed the only other chair in the room. "Why are names power?"

A line appeared between the demon's eyes, but he didn't respond.

He had no idea what to do or say. Jonathan had never interrogated anyone in his life. He glanced around the room again, hoping for inspiration. His gaze landed on a bucket of water. "When was the last time you had anything to eat or drink?"

The demon shrugged. "The big one sometimes feeds me."

Jonathan had no idea who the big one was supposed to be. To him, all the guys were big. "What do demons eat?"

"I'm half human, so anything you can, I suppose."

After coming to his feet, Jonathan moved to the bucket of water and peered inside. It looked clean. He checked but didn't see a cup anywhere. Jonathan motioned toward the bucket. "Is this what you've been drinking?"

A snort filled the air. "Are you joking? That's holy water."

Jonathan's gaze returned to the bucket. Moving slow, hoping to work up his courage, Jonathan traced the rim with the tip of his finger. No one talked to him about anything. Would he lose a finger if he touched the water? He should know the answer. Aggravation clawed at his brain. He was tired of being kept in the dark. Sometimes he half expected to wake up and find himself wrapped in cellophane. Jonathan didn't know if it was because he was the prince's mate or if the guys didn't see him as equal. Either way, he wondered how long it would be before he broke. Before he could change his mind, Jonathan dipped his finger in the water. Nothing happened. No burning flesh or trumpets sounding.

"You really expected to get burned, didn't you?"

Jonathan glanced over and met the demon's gaze. His eyes were no longer brown. They were gold. Jonathan couldn't draw a full breath. For a moment, they stared at each other before Jonathan looked away. It seemed weak for some reason, admitting he had no clue what he was about any longer, but he got the feeling this demon knew more about him than Jonathan knew about himself.

"It's Lire."

Their gaze met once more. "What?"

"My name," the demon said. "It's Lire."

Faolan, why are names power? Jonathan wasn't sure if Faolan would answer since it seemed the guys were hell-bent on keeping him in the dark. He was more than a little surprised when the vamp answered right away.

If you know a demon's name, you can summon it at any time.

"Jonathan," Jonathan said, hoping by giving Lire his name, he'd earn the demon's trust.

A low and sexy-sounding chuckle filled the air. Jonathan shook his head, trying to clear the haze the sound created. "That was an idiotic move, Jonathan."

Jonathan shook his head again as Lire said his name. The haze thickened, but Jonathan refused to show Lire any weakness. "No more so than you giving me your name, Lire." The fog cleared from Jonathan's mind as he said Lire's name. "Especially since you know I'll have to share it with my clansmen."

"True," Lire said, sounding as if it mattered not at all. "But I don't think you'll tell them."

Jonathan reclaimed his seat. "What makes you think so?" Jonathan asked, genuinely curious. He didn't think he would tell anyone either, but he wanted to hear why Lire didn't think he would.

Lire shrugged. "You call them your clansmen, yet you're different from them, and it has nothing to do with you being a new turn. They hold you apart, or you do.

Either way, you're an outsider here. I recognize the signs."

"Are you an outsider in your pack?" Jonathan asked instead of admitting how right Lire was.

Lire smiled. It was alluring and frightening. "I'm not sure there's such a thing as an insider in a demon pack. There's the top and the bottom. Those who lead and those who follow."

Jonathan leaned forward—fascinated. "Which are you? Do you lead or follow?"

Lire's smile slipped away. "I strive to do neither."

An unexpected wave of kinship washed over Jonathan. Lire was half human in a world of full-bloods. At least Jonathan had been turned by beings of his choosing. Lire had been born into a world of evil he'd never escape. That is, if he left here alive.

Jonathan swiped his palms on his

jeans, feeling useless. "Give me one detail I can share with my clansman—something of use, and I'll get you something to eat and some clean clothes."

"No, thank you," Lire said, surprising Jonathan. "Your show of kindness will only make going home feel all that much worse, especially once the torture begins. I'd like to think I won't tell the pack leaders what I told you, but I know better."

Jonathan swallowed, wishing he didn't care. "Then tell me something of no use, so you'll have something to tell them to make the torture stop."

Lire's smile reappeared, but this time, it was fake and brittle. "You know nothing of demons if you think giving them what they want will make them stop. Bending to a demon's will only makes them want to keep going, hoping they'll reshape you into something twisted."

"You're half demon. Are you the

same?"

At Jonathan's question, Lire's expression transformed, turning sultry. "I'm half Lilin-demon. It's definitely my place to twist you and make you want more."

He had no idea what that meant, but he could Google it later and not look like an idiot now. "Is that my one piece of useless info?"

Another sexy rumble of laughter filled the room. "No. I'm fairly certain your large friend has already figured that much out for himself."

"All my friends are big. You'll have to be more specific."

Lire's eyes flashed with humor. "Two are impervious to me because they belong to you. The ridiculous one with amethyst eyes has no heart to tempt. Who does that leave?" *Dougal.* "By the way, kudos on snagging two vampires. Your nights must be…" Lire paused and visibly inhaled before picking up where he left off. "…amazing."

They were, but not for the reason Lire thought. "Is there anything in particular you'd like to eat?"

"Low salt, please," Lire said with a laugh.

His words reminded Jonathan of his grandmother using salt to ward off demons when Jonathan had been a kid. His parents had called her crazy. Now, Jonathan wasn't so sure. "Will salt harm you?"

Lire smirked. "I'm only half demon. In small doses, I can take it. It burns going down, but then again, so do all the best things," he said with a wink.

Jonathan stood and headed for the door. Lire hadn't given him anything, but he wouldn't let the dude starve. He almost made it to the door before Lire called out, stopping him.

"The girls you've been tracking, hoping to find the pack; they're not dead. At least, not all of them."

Jonathan glanced over his shoulder, hoping Lire wouldn't see the journalist inside Jonathan, jumping for joy and planning its next move. "Thank you. I'll find you something to wear."

"Don't thank me, Jonathan," Lire said, continuously using Jonathan's name, as if trying to get in his head. "Sometimes being alive means less than nothing at all."

That was true. This time, Jonathan didn't wait for Lire to say more. He headed for the kitchen, running through the contents of their fridge in his mind. After deciding on a low sodium pasta dish and getting it started, Jonathan dipped inside the laundry room. He found a T-shirt and jeans he thought would fit Lire before returning to the kitchen. Jonathan almost made it without getting caught.

Dougal stepped into the kitchen. "Weren't you eating the last time I saw you?"

His gaze skirted away from Dougal's. "It's not for me."

"Cin and Faolan aren't here, and Niall doesn't like pasta."

"Yep," Jonathan said, trying hard not to look at Dougal.

Dougal moved closer. "Is all of this for our reluctant guest?" Dougal asked, nodding toward the clothes and food.

Jonathan's shoulders fell. "Yes."

Dougal relieved him of the plate and clothes. "I'll take it out there to him," the vamp said, shocking Jonathan before he remembered Lire's words about the big one. Curiosity ate at Jonathan, but he wouldn't ask.

Instead, he chose to give in gracefully. As long as Lire got what was promised to him, Jonathan didn't care who delivered. "That's fine."

"Good," Dougal said, sounding hard. "Because you need to take your ass out back and kick Niall out of his funk. He hasn't left his shop since you fed him this morning."

Aggravation made Jonathan's skin itch. Niall couldn't hide for the rest of their lives. Before he could call it back, Jonathan growled. "I'll take care of it."

With a nod, as if he took Jonathan at his word, Dougal headed for the garage. Jonathan headed out back. He hadn't been inside Niall's workspace before. For a full five minutes, Jonathan stood outside, wondering if he should knock. In the end, he barged in, refusing to give Niall time to turn him away. His steps slowed as he crossed the threshold. It was quiet inside. Knives and swords of every size and variety hung on the walls. Jonathan gave them a quick glance before searching for Niall. He found his mate, kicked back and asleep in a recliner.

A smile pulled at the corners of Jonathan's mouth. Niall looked ten times less intense while sleeping. After a quick search, Jonathan found a blanket. He moved slowly, hoping not to wake the man. When Niall didn't budge, Jonathan released the breath he hadn't known he'd been holding before claiming a hard-back chair across from him. The moment his ass hit the seat, the peace Jonathan experienced from being in his mate's presence slipped away. He wasn't wanted here. The only reason he was allowed to stay was because Niall was asleep. Cin only wanted to be with Jonathan when they were having sex. Niall never wanted to be around him. Jonathan had never felt more unwanted than he had since they'd turned him. He should go back inside and chat with the demon. At least the spawn hadn't made Jonathan feel as if his presence was unwelcome. Fuck. He'd forgotten to Google Lilin-demons.

"Lilin-demons are sex demons, and I always want to be with you."

Jonathan's gaze shot to Niall's. The vamp's golden irises always punched Jonathan in the chest. He couldn't explain it. No one bothered explaining it to him. Jonathan had never felt more lost. "I didn't mean to bother you." Sadness climbed up Jonathan's throat, choking him. "Dougal said you hadn't been inside all day. I just wanted to check on you. You can go back to sleep." Jonathan stood, intent on heading back inside. There was nothing for him here. There was nothing for him anywhere.

Niall held the cover up, opening his arms to Jonathan in a silent invitation to join him. "Your thoughts are louder than everyone else's when you're not guarding them."

For a moment, Jonathan chewed on his bottom lip, unsure of what to do. In the end, he couldn't resist Niall. This was the man who'd turned him. Jonathan would always feel lost without him. Niall moved over, making room for Jonathan. As Jonathan settled into his arms, Niall covered them with the blanket. The material still held the warmth of Niall's skin. Jonathan bit back a sigh. Later, he would look back on this moment with guilt. Right now, the itching inside his brain needed relief only Niall could give.

*

On one hip, with one leg thrown over Niall's, and his face buried in the crook of Niall's neck, Jonathan's breath fanned across Niall's throat. Niall should be uncomfortable. He wasn't. If he looked too closely at things, he should be guilt ridden. He wasn't. There was no peace any longer. Not for him. Not for anyone. He was used to the inner fury. Jonathan wasn't. Niall couldn't let it go on. The man thought Niall didn't want him around. He thought Cin only wanted him for sex. Niall had never been more furious at everyone, including himself. There had to be some middle ground. He couldn't find it. So, instead, he held Jonathan's hand against his chest and listened to his steady breathing. Niall let the sound of Jonathan's heart beat fill his ears and drown out all other noise. He could feel Jonathan's exhaustion. It matched his.

"Tell me about your day," Jonathan said against his skin.

Niall's eyes fell closed at the sensation of the man's lips brushing his throat. He relaxed deeper into the chair. "I'm making a new sword."

"What's it look like?"

"Like a sword." Jonathan chuckled at Niall's answer. The sound vibrated against Niall's chest, making him smile. He held his mate tighter. "What's wrong?" Niall asked. "I mean, besides everything."

He felt Jonathan's lips shape into a smile against his neck. "I think that pretty much covers it. Is it okay if I just be still for a minute and hold you? Life isn't as loud when I'm with you."

Niall pressed his lips to Jonathan's head and breathed in the man's scent. "Of course."

"Everyone's helpless anger is suffocating me," Jonathan said, sounding half awake.

"Impotency pisses people off." It had been so long since Niall found anything funny, even he was surprised by the heavy humor in his tone.

"I doubt that's a problem you suffer."

Niall toyed with Jonathan's fingers. For the first time, outside a dream, they felt ensconced and separate from the clan. They were intimate and Jonathan was his. "No. If anything, I might go blind from touching myself too much."

Jonathan's low laughter caressed Niall's skin. As if his dick needed to prove Niall wasn't a liar, it stirred at the sensation. "You're ridiculous."

"I'm serious. Don't take this the wrong way, but you're the kinkiest person I've ever met. The inside of your head is a dirty place. You've turned the inside of my mind into a twenty-four-seven porn station. I've lived a long time, and I've never met anyone as willing to do or try anything as you are."

He could smell Jonathan's blush. His lust hit an all-time high the instant Jonathan's blood rushed to the surface of his skin. "Sorry. I can try keeping you blocked if I'm too much."

"Hell, no. I don't want that. You have no idea how boring it is to live forever. Everything becomes tedious as hell. Since meeting you, I haven't been bored for a second, and yes, that includes the six years there was no chance you'd be mine." Niall realized what he'd said. Jonathan didn't comment. Niall breathed a sigh of relief. "Thank you for not calling me on saying that."

He felt more than saw Jonathan shrug. "I know what you meant."

Did he? Niall wasn't so sure, but it didn't matter. "Go to sleep, sweet one. I can feel your exhaustion."

"Meet me there," Jonathan said, sounding more asleep than awake.

"I always do." And it wouldn't stop. That knowledge scared the hell out of Niall. As long as they both lived, Niall wouldn't stop, and he wasn't sure how far he'd go before the end. He probed at Jonathan's brain. The tension in Niall's shoulders didn't relent until the man in his arms finally fell asleep. Once he felt Jonathan slip into his dream stage, Niall spent a moment eyeing him. Jonathan always looked sweet and innocent. Niall's lips pulled at the corners. He loved holding this man.

Jonathan shifted his sleep. His hand came to rest on Niall's erection. Niall sucked in a hiss. The heat radiating from Jonathan's palm had Niall resisting the urge to grind himself against Jonathan's hand. To keep from doing something idiotic, he closed his eyes and slipped inside Jonathan's dream. The instant the images in Jonathan's head became clear, Niall marveled over the clarity of it all. Jonathan was easily one of the strongest Seers he'd ever encountered. He didn't understand why his mate didn't seem to recognize how much he could do.

They were standing in the kitchen. Jonathan leaned against the counter with his arms crossed over his chest. It couldn't have been more apparent he'd been waiting for Niall. At his arrival, Jonathan met his gaze. Niall stopped breathing. Jonathan had never looked at him the way he did now. Niall took a step in the man's direction. Jonathan straightened away from the counter. They met halfway.

"It's only a dream," Niall said, needing Jonathan.

"I'll take it," Jonathan said, capturing Niall's mouth.

Niall was older, taller, twice Jonathan's size and ten times his strength. None of those things mattered because Jonathan made him weak. Their kiss was desperate because they were. Niall grabbed two handfuls of Jonathan's ass and lifted him from his feet. Jonathan wrapped his legs around Niall's waist as if they'd done this a thousand times. He stumbled through the kitchen and into the living room without giving up Jonathan's mouth. Once he made it to the couch, he toppled onto the piece of furniture with Jonathan trapped beneath him. Every place their bodies touched, burned. Niall wanted to bury himself inside Jonathan. This wasn't about sex. He could have Jonathan in this dream, and maybe it would satisfy some part of him. Niall needed more than Jonathan's body. He needed to feel the man's heart.

With a tug, Niall yanked Jonathan's shirt upward, baring the man's chest. He tore his mouth away from the delicious way Jonathan sucked his bottom lip and pressed his forehead to where Jonathan's heart beat steady. Niall's eyes fell closed as he inhaled Jonathan's scent and let the rhythm soothe him. The sound filled his ears, sounding like a drum. His lips brushed Jonathan's sternum, worshipping the man's life-giving force.

He'd never been more grateful for another person's existence the way he was this man's. Sex was a good thing. Not being alone in the world was amazing. That was what Jonathan gave him. Niall could ignore what the man did to his body. He couldn't hide from what Jonathan's existence did to his mind.

Jonathan's fingers ran through his hair, as if soothing Niall. "I wish you would tell me what you need. Don't hide."

A loud clicking noise snatched Niall from the dream of being in Jonathan's arms. His eyes flew open and his gaze shot to the door. Before his uninvited guest could make an appearance, Niall dissipated and reappeared standing next to his workbench, leaving Jonathan alone in the chair. He wiped the sweat from his brow on his shoulder as he picked up a knife he'd been sharpening earlier and pretended to inspect it. His body ached and his mind was a mess. Now wasn't the time for anyone to talk to him, but there was no avoiding it.

Cin stepped into the room. His gaze swept over Jonathan's sleeping form before coming to rest on Niall. Niall didn't doubt for a second he could see it all—Niall's desire. The way he was slowly dying. There wasn't an ounce of condemnation in Cin's eyes. Niall didn't know if that piece of information made things better or worse. Without a word, Cin crossed the room and stood over Jonathan. "I don't understand why he sleeps so much," Cin said while claiming the same chair Niall had found Jonathan in earlier.

Niall kept his back to Cin, hoping the man wouldn't see the lingering lust clinging to Niall's skin. "For the same reason as a newborn bairn. He can't help it. His body is still adjusting to the massive energy his new form burns as it constantly regenerates cells. Creating perfection is hard work," Niall said, wanting to bite off his tongue the second he went too far.

"He was already perfect," Cin said, keeping his voice low and his gaze locked on Jonathan. "That's one of the many reasons I never wanted to turn him. I knew I couldn't improve on what he was born with."

"Or maybe you never wanted to turn him because you didn't want the responsibility," Niall said before he could stop himself.

Cin's gaze snapped to his. "If you have something to say to me, say it."

Niall shrugged. "It's curious to me how you stay gone more now than ever before."

"In case you've forgotten, we have a demon pack growing larger and bolder than ever before," Cin said, refusing to take the bait and give Niall the fight he was itching for.

Without thought, Niall slammed down his knife and narrowed his eyes at Cin. "I haven't forgotten, but Jonathan needs you here and not just for sex."

That did it. Cin came to his feet. His fury-filled gaze held Niall's. "You're the one who disappeared for two months without a word."

"No doubt, while I was gone, you pulled the same shit you are now. Has Jonathan learned anything about our world or have you been too busy pulling away and hoping you don't get hurt? Hell, he didn't even know I was his prince until today."

The clicking of a door closing brought Niall's head around. The chair was empty. Jonathan was gone. Tilting his chin toward the ceiling, Niall prayed for Goddess Celeste to take mercy on him. Surely no other vampire had failed their mate the way Niall was failing his.

"Niall, I can't—"

"Please, Cin," Niall said, cutting him off. "You begged me to save him and I did. Just leave me be." He no longer knew who he was the angriest with, but Niall very much feared it was himself.

*

Jonathan was nowhere to be found. The house was empty and Jonathan's mind was shut. No matter how he begged and pleaded, Jonathan wouldn't let him inside his head. He hadn't gone in search of Jonathan and Niall looking for a fight. Cin had hoped, when he found them together, maybe they could talk about things. Every time he tried, things looked a little more hopeless. Niall would never admit to needing them, while Jonathan felt abandoned by them both.

Cin found Faolan in the kitchen. He grabbed the man before he could get away. "Have you seen Jonathan?"

"Aye," Faolan said with a nod. "He walked through here a minute ago, holding his laptop, and saying he had shit to do."

Cin ground his back teeth to keep from screaming. "Where did he go?"

Faolan shrugged. "No clue. He said he didn't want to be bothered with anyone else today. I took him at his word and let him be." Faolan slapped Cin across the back as if he wasn't a single a breath away from losing his life. "You're always gone these days. If you want your space, then you should let the boy have his peace. It's nae as if you've been caring what he gets up to any other time."

Before Cin had a chance to rip out Faolan's heart, the vamp disappeared, leaving Cin alone with his fury. It seemed everyone was of the same mind. He was the ass who was never around. No one saw the truth. Jonathan and Niall needed time together without his interference. If not, they might never see the truth.

Chapter 5

This time, Jonathan didn't hesitate entering Lire's space inside the garage. He found Lire still seated in the center of the room, in the god-awful chair, but looking a little less ragged than he had earlier in the day. With his feet crossed at the ankles and his arms crossed over his chest, Lire looked bored off his ass. Jonathan held up his laptop and motioned toward the empty chair in the room.

"Do you mind if I join you?"

Lire waved toward the seat as if inviting Jonathan to stay. "It's your house."

Since Jonathan didn't feel that was true, he let the comment pass without response. After snagging the empty chair, he carried it to the table where the bucket of water sat. He set up his laptop. Jonathan opened a blank document and started a research list, treating this demon issue the way he would any story. He needed to concentrate on anything at all other than the mess his life had become, so he typed a list that wouldn't mean anything to anyone other than him.

Spawn

Demons

Lilin-demon

Young women

Tourist towns: Tortola, Bahamas, research others.

Common factors: age

Not dead: supposedly

"May I ask you a question?"

Jonathan glanced up from his list and

focused on Lire at the demon's inquiry. "Sure."

"Why are you here, hanging out with me—a demon, the same creature as the one responsible for your turn—instead of spending time with your abundance of men?"

A knot formed in Jonathan's gut. "How do you know a demon was responsible for my turn?"

A line appeared between Lire's eyes, as if he didn't know what to make of Jonathan. "I was there when you were attacked. Why do you think your dark prince spent months tracking me? He wasn't about to let me slip away. I'm the only link he has to capturing the one responsible for hurting you."

Jonathan dropped his gaze to the computer screen, hoping to hide his reaction to Lire's words. It seemed everyone knew Niall was a prince, except for Jonathan—his mate. "You're not the one responsible, are you?" Jonathan asked, even though he knew Lire wasn't. That day, as he'd slid to the floor, Jonathan had looked into the eyes of evil. He'd never forget the face of the demon who'd stolen his life—never.

"You know I am not," Lire said, as if he could read Jonathan's thoughts.

Jonathan flashed Lire a quick grin. "Then what does it matter if I sit with you? You must be bored to tears. Not to mention, I wanted to make sure you'd gotten the food and clothes I promised."

Lire's eyes changed colors while his face remained clear of all emotion. "You should go back inside, Jonathan."

"I don't want to, Lire," Jonathan said.

Two could play at the game of intentional name usage.

"Your clan intends to kill me. There's no circumstance where I walk away from here. As soon as they have the information they seek, my life will come to an end. You're not like them. The more time you spend with me, the more my death will haunt you. Please go back inside and forget I exist."

"No."

Lire's eyes stopped changing, settling on blue. "Do you think I'm lying?"

Despite the heavy topic, Jonathan smiled. "No, but going back inside is a real inconvenience for me. I've already got my laptop all set up and everything. So, really, it would just be easier for me if you wouldn't tell them anything they want to know until I can figure out how to save you."

A smile exploded across Lire's face. "You're an odd man. Even though there's no hope of my life being spared, I'm grateful you'd think to try." Lire straightened in his seat. "You never answered my question. Why are you hiding out here?"

Jonathan set his elbows on the table before resting his chin on his fists. He held Lire's stare as he tried to decide what or how much to say. Finally, he chose to be vague. "I guess, in a way, I'm a prisoner here too."

Lire nodded, looking unfazed by the confession. "As the prince's mate, your clan would keep you sheltered from harm, I imagine. I'm sure it gets quite tiresome."

The more Lire spoke, the more Jonathan wanted to know. He'd always possessed an insatiable need for information. "How do you know I'm the prince's mate?" Jonathan stopped short of admitting even he hadn't known before that morning.

Lire motioned toward the designs painting the room. "All this is meant to keep me prisoner, but this doesn't do much to bind my powers."

Instead of looking like an idiot, Jonathan minimized his document and opened his web browser.

Lire's laughter filled the room. "Google can't tell you what powers I have, Jonathan. Each demon is unique, and that's a man-made system."

Jonathan's cheeks burned.

Lire's expression went from amused to heated in an instant. "You're not very good at keeping your innocence hidden."

"You're not very good at keeping your nice hidden."

Lire's expression hardened. "I'm not nice."

"I'm not innocent," Jonathan shot back.

Lire sat forward in his seat, holding Jonathan captivated by his ever-changing eye color. "Touch my hand, and I'll show you everything."

A snort escaped Jonathan before he could call it back. "I'm sure. Right before you kill me."

Lire's expression never changed. "No games. I won't hurt you. Touch my hand," he repeated, cajoling Jonathan with his voice.

Some ridiculous form of fuck-it-all rose inside Jonathan. Dougal had sworn

Jonathan would be safe thanks to their ancient symbols. He might not trust Lire, but he did trust his clan. They wouldn't have asked for his help if they weren't one hundred percent certain Lire couldn't harm him. Of course, they'd also been just as sure Jonathan had enough sense to stay out of the circle drawn around Lire's chair. Shows what they know about my level of good sense, Jonathan thought as he came to his feet.

Before he could change his mind, Jonathan crossed the room. Lire watched his every move—like a lion stalking its prey. Still, Jonathan didn't slow. As he stepped across the lines drawn on the floor, the air rippled, as if he'd walked through an invisible wall. Lire stood. There wasn't an ounce of triumph written on his face. Yet the first hint of real fear still settled on Jonathan's shoulders. Slumped in his seat, Lire hadn't looked anywhere near as imposing as he did now, towering over Jonathan.

Too late, Jonathan questioned his judgment. Even his late-to-the-game common sense didn't stop Jonathan from accepting Lire's outstretched hand. Their palms met. The demon's skin was even hotter than Jonathan imagined it would be. Lire lightly squeezed Jonathan's hand, and nothing happened. A wicked glint lit Lire's eyes. A single red rose appeared in Lire's free hand. He passed it Jonathan's way.

"You're right," Lire said as Jonathan accepted his gift. "Innocence isn't your issue. You're touched in the head."

"Possibly," Jonathan said as he brought the flower to his nose. "But this encounter has told me more than you intended, I believe."

Lire's lips turned up in the corners, becoming almost as wicked as his eyes. "Do tell."

Before Jonathan could decide how much he should admit, the door opened. Panic overtook Jonathan. He glanced around, hoping for an exit to save him. It didn't matter who it was, Jonathan was doomed. If anyone found him inside Lire's demon trap, today would be the day he'd end up locked in his room and wrapped in cellophane. Lire squeezed his hand, pulling Jonathan's attention his way. The demon touched his finger to his lips, gesturing for Jonathan to be quiet.

Jonathan nodded.

Lire leaned close and touched his lips to the shell of Jonathan's ear. He whispered something in Latin. Jonathan's skin tingled—like ants crawled over his body. "Head for the door," Lire said. His

128

lips brushed Jonathan's ear with each word. "I promise no one will see you."

Dougal stepped into the room.

Lire sat.

Jonathan did as Lire said and moved for the door.

Dougal's eyes never wavered from Lire's. Jonathan didn't understand what Lire had done, but Dougal couldn't see him. He slowed as he passed Dougal, half expecting to be caught. Dougal turned his head as if he felt a shift in the air. Jonathan held his breath and froze.

Dougal motioned toward the table. Jonathan had to jump back to keep from getting hit. "I see you've had company."

Jonathan glanced over. His gaze landed on his laptop. He tilted his chin toward the ceiling and threw a silent fit.

He was such an idiot. In his panic to not get caught with Lire, he'd completely forgotten about his computer.

"Your friend has been full of questions for me today," Lire said, sounding bored by it all.

Dougal took a step toward the laptop. "Let's see what the genius in our bunch has to say about you."

Jonathan glanced Lire's way. Panic owned him. He couldn't let Dougal see his notes. Lire wasn't good. Jonathan had felt the man's darkness the moment their hands met, but neither was Lire evil. Jonathan couldn't let his clan kill Lire. If they saw his notes and realized how much Jonathan had learned, Lire might not make it until Jonathan could find a way to save him.

Lire met his gaze and winked. "Don't

be tiresome, Blondy," Lire said, snapping his fingers. The computer popped, and the screen went black. "If you have questions, ask them yourself."

Jonathan's shoulders sagged with relief. He inched toward the door once more. Once he reached it, another problem arose. There was no way he could open it without drawing attention to himself. He glanced Lire's way again, searching for help. He didn't know how Lire could save him this time, but he knew the demon had magic. Jonathan would venture to say Lire was more powerful than anyone realized. Lire's gaze flickered in Jonathan's direction. He covered his mouth as if hiding a yawn. Jonathan's skin tingled again.

"Here's your genius now," Lire said. "You can question him on our chat."

Dougal glanced behind him, looking

more than a little surprised Jonathan had gotten the drop on him. "You're back."

"Just long enough to grab my laptop," Jonathan said, motioning toward the device as if Dougal might not have seen it sitting there.

The huge vamp's eyebrows rose. "Is there a reason you're carrying a rose around?"

Jonathan glanced down and blinked. He'd never been a good liar. He was a journalist at heart and dealt in facts. "I forgot I had it," Jonathan said, deciding to go with his strength—honesty.

Dougal shook his head. "You're a verra odd man."

Lire snorted.

Jonathan's shoulders fell. "That seems to be the general consensus," Jonathan said as he moved to gather his laptop.

"Be careful," Dougal said, nodding toward the computer. "Our guest did something to it. You shouldn't leave anything alone with him."

He didn't meet Dougal's gaze. It was best for everyone if he got out of there as quickly as possible before he gave himself away. "I'm sure it'll be fine. If not, it's old and needs replacing anyhow."

Lire chuckled. It was as sexy as it was evil sounding. "I gave it an update."

Dougal snorted. "More likely, he gave it a virus."

"I only give viruses the fun way," Lire said, keeping Dougal engaged.

"There's literally nothing sexy about what you just said."

Jonathan made a break for it while

they were distracted. He didn't breathe an easy breath until the door closed behind him. The moment it did, the rose transformed into a slip of paper. For a full minute, Jonathan stared it—transfixed. It was a bit frightening how powerful Lire was, even with safeguards in place.

He tucked the laptop under his arm and unfolded the paper. There was one piece of information scratched inside, and it meant everything.

Port of Southern Louisiana.

Jonathan now held Lire's life in his hands.

Chapter 6

Cin found Jonathan sitting quietly in the shadows on the back patio. He wouldn't have spotted him if not for the glow of the man's laptop.

Jonathan glanced up when Cin came to stand over him. "Hey, baby."

The tension in Cin's shoulders slipped away at Jonathan's greeting. "I've been looking for you."

Jonathan's forehead furrowed in the sexy way Cin couldn't resist. "I thought you'd be out searching the docks."

Cin shrugged. "One night off won't change anything. Besides, I'd rather be with you." After urging Jonathan forward in the lounge chair, Cin climbed in behind him and wrapped both arms around Jonathan's waist. "What are you working on?" Jonathan tilted his screen so Cin could see it. Cin rested his chin on Jonathan's shoulder and read. "Port of Southern Louisiana. Are you on to something?"

"Yes and no," Jonathan said with a shrug. "I had a chat with our guest today."

"I don't like you going near him," Cin said, cutting Jonathan off without thought. He'd told himself he would let Jonathan in, but questioning a demon—even a spawn—was more than Cin could take.

"Too bad," Jonathan shot back, showing the fire Cin had never been able to resist. He glanced over his shoulder, meeting Cin's gaze. "No one owns me, Cin. My choices might be to stay here or starve, but those are still choices."

Cin heard what Jonathan didn't say.

The man might very well choose to starve if pushed. The first wave of hope Cin had experienced in ages rose inside him at Jonathan's defiance. This rolling over and hating himself that Jonathan had been showing was slowly killing Cin. He wanted his Jonathan back. His hold tightened on Jonathan's waist. He pressed his lips to the man's cheek and chuckled.

"Point taken. So, why Louisiana?"

"Because that's the info I got from our guest today."

Surprise had Cin blinking like an idiot at Jonathan's answer. "Seriously? Is that all he said?"

"The only thing of consequence," Jonathan said, sounding distracted. "The problem is, we can't find anything here, and we only have twenty-two miles to search. Port of Southern Louisiana is one hundred and seventy-two miles on both banks of the Mississippi river. It's impossible."

Getting sucked in, Cin added his thoughts. "Try searching for places with a high missing persons count."

Jonathan snorted. "You do realize, New Orleans is part of that one-hundred-and-seventy-two-mile stretch. Countless people have gone missing from that area, and that doesn't include the homeless population. There's no way to keep track of their whereabouts."

The passion and drive was back in Jonathan's voice. He was on the case now. Too late, Cin realized this was what he'd been stealing from Jonathan by keeping him secluded. All the qualities he'd fallen for when he'd fallen in love with Jonathan were showing themselves once more, making Cin realize the depth of his mistakes.

"You know I love you, right?" Cin asked, incapable of letting Jonathan continue to believe otherwise for another second.

"Yes."

Cin winced. Jonathan's agreement sounded more like a question than an affirmation. Cin grabbed the laptop from Jonathan's hands and set it aside before pulling Jonathan tighter against his chest. Sometimes, Cin thought, if he held Jonathan tight enough, the man would finally understand how much he meant.

"I keep hoping we'll find this pack, and then you and I can get lost for a little while. Maybe even talk Niall into going with us somewhere away from everything."

"Is that really what you want or are you saying what you think I want to hear?"

A derisive-sounding snort left Cin before he could call it back. "Since the turn, I couldn't even begin to guess what you want any longer."

He felt Jonathan take a deep breath. Instead of flying into a rage, as Cin expected, he relaxed into Cin's hold. "I can't tell when I'm hiding my thoughts." Relief washed over Cin at the confession. He'd thought Jonathan was keeping him out on purpose. It would make sense he couldn't control it. "If I concentrate hard, I can put up a wall. Otherwise, whatever happens in there is out of my control." Jonathan laughed as if he thought he sounded ridiculous. "I didn't realize how much all of you depend on hearing my thoughts. None of you would ever make it as a human. No one ever knows what anyone's thinking. You have to take things on trust and faith."

"I trust you," Cin said without missing a beat.

The humor in Jonathan's voice died away. "Maybe you shouldn't."

Cin shook his head before touching his lips to Jonathan's nape. "You're so young. There's a great big gray area out there you haven't been introduced to yet."

Jonathan snorted. "I don't even know what that's supposed to mean."

Niall appeared beside the chair. He seemed wary of his welcome. "May I join you?"

Jonathan moved his legs and Niall sat on the end of the lounge chair. Once he was settled, he urged Jonathan's feet into his lap. Still, the cautious glint didn't leave his eyes.

"Did you finish your sword?" Jonathan

asked.

Niall's shoulders relaxed.

Cin hid his smile. Jonathan always seemed to know exactly what to say to set Niall at ease.

"I did. Maybe you can check it out tomorrow?"

"I'd like that."

Cin held his breath. The three of them were together. They weren't fighting or feeding. All he could do now was hope neither man stormed off.

"Jonathan got some info out of our reluctant guest," Cin said, hoping to keep things heading in the right direction.

Niall's eyebrows rose. "Really?"

Jonathan nodded. "It's not much, considering, but the pack is somewhere near Port of Southern Louisiana."

"Damn. That's a huge area to search."

"I'd like to keep questioning him." Jonathan's words came out rushed, as if he expected to be denied.

"Of course," Niall said, sounding like it was a given. "You've gotten more out of him in one day than we have in over a month. As long as you don't cross the circle surrounding him, you should be safe."

He felt Jonathan tense. Cin automatically tried to read his thoughts at the move. Before he made any headway, Jonathan let his feelings fly. "I'd like to be the only one questioning him. No more torture. Today has proven that method won't work on him, and he might decide not to tell me anything else if you four are taking turns hurting him after I leave."

Niall massaged Jonathan's legs,

looking lost in thought. Cin didn't think the man was aware of touching Jonathan. Finally, Niall sighed. "Honestly, I'm fine to leave you to it, since I'm obviously wasting my time. I'll let the others know to stay away as well."

The tension bled from Jonathan at Niall's answer. Cin couldn't decide why it was so important to him. "Thank you."

"You know he's evil, right?" Niall asked, searching Jonathan's face with his gaze. "Demons are deceivers. He'll say anything to gain your trust."

"You don't have to worry over me," Jonathan said, sounding so sure it was impossible to doubt him. "A demon killed me not too long ago. I won't be an easy target."

Niall smiled. It was sweet. Cin's chest tightened at the sight. He couldn't remember the last time Niall smiled and meant it. Niall continued to rub Jonathan's legs as if he'd forgotten anyone else was there. "I trust you not to rip our hearts out by getting yourself hurt."

Cin's heart stopped before slamming against the wall of his chest. Niall had definitely included Cin in that statement. It was the first time Niall had said anything that gave Cin hope. Cin pounced on it before Niall had time to shut them out again.

"So, that's settled. You should come to bed with us."

Jonathan stiffened in his hold but didn't speak up, withdrawing the offer. The silence filling the air said a lot about how hard Niall and Jonathan were trying to hide their thoughts.

"I'm sorry. What?"

Cin had a hard time hiding his smile. He couldn't imagine how it looked because it felt evil even to him. "You should tell whatever dark thoughts you've been having to go fuck themselves. Stop pretending this isn't what you want and come to bed with us."

Niall looked away. Cin stared at his profile, watching the muscles in the man's jaw flex. He wondered how anyone could ever mistake him for anything less than royalty. Niall gave off the most powerful vibe of anyone he'd ever met. No matter how angry he looked now, Niall hadn't stopped running his hands over Jonathan's legs. If Jonathan had taken a single breath since Cin made his offer, he hadn't heard it happen.

Cin dropped his voice, trying not to spook Niall. He was a runner. "You don't have to do anything this first time. We could just turn off the lights and hold each other."

Niall finally looked over and met Jonathan's gaze. The fury in the other man's eyes took Cin back. "I'm sorry I turned you so you could spend eternity with a mate more than willing to share you. If you were with me, I never could." Niall disappeared before Cin had time to explain.

A sharp pain stabbed Cin through the heart. It was so intense he couldn't tell if it was his or Jonathan's.

Jonathan stood. He wouldn't meet Cin's gaze. "Go after him. That's what you want."

"I want you," Cin said, hearing the aggravation in his voice. He couldn't temper it.

Jonathan stared straight ahead, hiding his thoughts and emotions.

"There's still two hours before dawn. Go after him. I'll see you at bedtime, as always." Without another word, Jonathan scooped his laptop from the ground and walked away. He needed a new plan. It was time for drastic measures.

*

After plugging his laptop in to charge, Jonathan headed for the kitchen. He grabbed Lire a few bottles of water.

Don't think.

He spotted a box of prepackaged cupcakes and grabbed those too. With his hands full, he couldn't rub the spot in the center of his chest that was slowly killing him.

Don't think.

The second he stepped inside the garage, the tension drained from his shoulders. Work. He had a project to busy his mind. The most Lire could do was kill him. Jonathan was certain everyone else was trying to destroy him. This time, he found Lire pacing.

He turned at Jonathan's arrival. "You're back. Don't you ever sleep?"

A snort escaped Jonathan. "Everyone else accuses me of sleeping too much."

Lire resumed his pacing. "You're depressed. People sleep a lot when they're sad."

Rather than taking Lire's bait, Jonathan moved to the edge of the circle and held up the water. "I brought some things for you."

Lire's mouth lifted in one corner, but he didn't stop pacing. "You realize I don't need any of that to survive, right?"

Jonathan tossed the water bottles and cupcakes inside and walked away. "That's fine. I won't bother next time." With his hands free, Jonathan gave in to temptation. He rubbed the center of his chest. Never in his life had he been more useless. He couldn't help Niall. Cin was hell-bent on forcing things. He knew next to nothing of the world he now lived in. The demons were no closer to being found. Even Lire didn't need his help.

"I said I didn't need it," Lire said, picking up the water. "I didn't say I didn't want it."

"Whatever." Jonathan heard the petulance in his tone. He was beyond caring.

"Jonathan." At his name, Jonathan met Lire's gaze. The man's eyes were gold again. "Thank you."

Jonathan dipped his chin. He recognized Lire wasn't one who thanked many people.

"Ask your questions," Lire said, cracking open the water. "You'll never learn anything about this world you've been thrust into if you don't ask."

A small smile tugged at Jonathan's lips

before a bark of laughter escaped.

Lire's forehead furrowed. "What's so funny?"

"I never thought the day would come when a demon would be more willing to talk to me than my mate. What a fucking mess my life has become," Jonathan said with a shake of his head. He sighed, trying to let it go. "It doesn't matter. How are you holding up in there?"

Lire didn't answer. Instead, he continued to drink his water while silently eyeing Jonathan. Once he polished off the water, Lire set the bottle aside. He waited until he'd reclaimed his chair before speaking. "Do you know how to bring two men to their knees? You get on yours," Lire said, answering his question before Jonathan had time. "If you're the one in control, then they'll be helpless. As long as you let either of them remain in charge, you'll always be at their mercy."

Jonathan thought there might be some good advice in there somewhere. He didn't feel like deciphering it right now.

"How old are you?" he asked instead.

"That's a rude question. You should guess and flatter me."

Jonathan eyed Lire for a moment before answering. "Thirty-two."

Lire smiled. "Close. I mean, I was thirty-two in 1605, so you weren't completely wrong."

"Seriously? But you're half human."

"And?" Lire asked, sounding genuinely curious to hear why Jonathan thought it mattered.

Jonathan shrugged. "I don't know. Shouldn't the human side of you age?"

"A single drop of supernatural blood will overpower any human aspects of your anatomy. Think about it. You were born human. Does it matter now?"

"Yes," Jonathan said without having to think about it. "I might be a vampire, but I can't do everything vampires can do, because I wasn't born a vampire. For example, I can't dissipate. If I want to get anywhere fast, I still have to drive there. The sun doesn't bother me at all. It stands to reason, even though you were born half demon, you'd still have some human traits."

Lire tapped his chin, being obnoxious in his attempts at thinking things over. "Well, I didn't kill you or use you to escape the one time you stepped inside my circle, so there's that."

Everything about Lire fascinated Jonathan. He loved learning about new things. In truth, he'd be every bit as excited to learn about life as a vampire too.

Unfortunately, he had to learn about that through trial and error since no one ever told him anything. Lire was always willing to talk to him. "So, you mean to tell me, if you were full demon, you would've killed me?"

"Why does a serial killer kill people?" Lire asked instead of answering.

Jonathan turned the question over in his mind. "I guess it could be for several reasons. Schizophrenia. Past child abuse. Really any number of mental disorders."

Lire shook his head as if he found Jonathan foolish. "Good people search for a reason behind every terrible act without understanding evil doesn't need an excuse. It's cold and empty. It exists for no reason other than destruction. Just as you struggle to understand how anyone could callously cut someone's life short, evil doesn't understand why you won't." Lire swiped his hand through the air, as if washing away his words. "But that's not what you asked."

"In a way, you answered my question," Jonathan said, lifting one shoulder in a half shrug. "If you were full demon, you would've killed me for no reason other than you could."

"Perhaps," Lire said, as if willing to debate. "Being half human doesn't lessen my dark nature. Instead, it adds a calculating side. If I'd killed you, Blondy would've killed me, and I like not being dead. Seriously, does no one sleep around here?" Lire asked, sounding as if he was done talking for the day.

Jonathan shrugged. "As far as I've seen, no one has a schedule. They just sleep whenever. There's no going to bed at night—or day. No one turns out the lights, letting the house go silent. I don't think

I've slept a full eight hours in one sitting since the turn."

"Aren't you tired, Jonathan?"

As Lire said his name, Jonathan's eyelids grew heavy. A yawn escaped. He was more exhausted than he'd ever been in his life.

Lire pointed toward the corner of the room. "There's a cot over there. You should sleep, Jonathan."

Another wave of weakness overcame him. He blinked at the corner. Jonathan was certain there hadn't been a cot in the room earlier. He was too tired to think straight.

"Okay," Jonathan said. Lire's suggestion sounded better by the minute. He could close his eyes for a little while. No one would bother him out here. Not that anyone was looking for him. The cot welcomed him. It was more comfortable than Jonathan expected. The instant his head hit the pillow, the world went dark.

Chapter 7

The sensation of ants crawling on his skin ripped Jonathan from the best sleep he'd had in ages. Dougal strolled through the room, headed for Lire.

"Stay the fook out of my dreams."

Jonathan opened his mouth, intent on announcing his presence. No sound emerged. He tried again. Nothing happened. It took him a second to realize the sensation that had awoken him was Lire hiding his presence. This time, he'd also stolen Jonathan's voice. His muscles weakened as if sleep tried pulling him under. Jonathan fought it. Dougal wore nothing except a ragged-looking kilt. If Jonathan had thought the man was beautiful clothed, it was nothing compared to the man half nude.

Without missing a step, Dougal crossed the lines of Lire's demon trap. "I've told you before, I don't want you in my head."

Are you determined to fight me and stay awake, Jonathan? Very well. I can't dampen my nature to spare you.

Jonathan shook his head, trying to dispel Lire's voice from his mind.

"I'm starving," Lire said, sounding turned on and making Jonathan's stomach cramp with want.

Dougal snagged the front of Lire's shirt and pulled the demon to his feet. "Get out of my head."

"It's not all me," Lire said as he raked his fingernails slowly down Dougal's back. "You just don't want to admit it."

A sound Jonathan had never heard before escaped Dougal. It was pain and lust. A tortured man on the edge of orgasm with no hope of relief.

"Give me what I need, Blondy. You swore you wouldn't let me starve."

159

Jonathan couldn't look away from the scene taking place across the room. He should close his eyes. Knowing it didn't make Jonathan turn his head. Niall was right about Jonathan's perversions. He couldn't look away.

"Goddamn you," Dougal swore, snagging the back of Lire's head.

"God doesn't look my way," Lire said, capturing Dougal's mouth.

The air thickened. Jonathan tried catching his breath. He didn't think he'd ever seen anything as hot as the way the muscles in Dougal's back rolled as Lire's fingers dug in, leaving indentions. Lire sat, bringing Dougal with him. Dougal straddled the man's hips.

"Damn, Blondy. You're not wearing anything underneath this." His hands slid beneath Dougal's kilt as he made the claim. "You're too used to being in charge," Lire said, nipping at Dougal's collarbone.

Dougal's head fell back. His panting breaths filled the air as he gave Lire more access to his throat. "Has anyone ever been inside you, sexy? Or are you always the one feeling that heat tightening on your cock?"

"No one controls me," Dougal said, obviously trying to hang on to some form of reality.

"I do," Lire growled, taking the last threads away from Dougal. "I'm about to push my way inside you. It'll hurt, but you'll let me anyway, because you want it. You want me. You want what I can do for you."

As Lire made his claims, his hands moved beneath Dougal's kilt. Jonathan couldn't see what the demon was doing, but he could guess. His hands balled into fists as he fought not to stroke his cock. Whatever spell Lire weaved around Dougal, Jonathan wasn't immune.

Now's the time, Jonathan. Sleep and bring your men to their knees.

At Lire's claim, the world slipped away.

*

He felt Jonathan the instant the man slipped inside his dreams. Niall had been determined to stay away tonight and let the man have time alone with Cin. Now Jonathan was here. Niall couldn't draw a full breath. The room shimmered, becoming his shop. A breeze touched his shins. Niall dropped his gaze. He was wearing a kilt. It was the one belonging to his family too, as if Jonathan had seen it somewhere before.

A low chuckle escaped him. "I haven't worn a kilt in years."

Jonathan appeared. His hot gaze raked Niall's body. "I had a sudden burning desire to see you in one."

162

Niall's mouth went dry. Jonathan had never looked at him before the way he did now, even after feeding. This was more. Niall wondered if he should run for his life. "You have a great imagination," Niall said, hoping to temper his desire. "This is the exact kilt my family wore."

"It's time to be quiet, Niall," Jonathan said, cutting him off. Niall snapped his teeth together. He'd definitely never seen this side of Jonathan, but he liked it. That didn't mean he intended to be quiet.

"You've never visited my dreams. It's always the other way around."

Jonathan's mouth covered his, stopping Niall from saying another word. His hand snaked up Niall's kilt, encircling Niall's dick. The man did a damn good job of stealing Niall's voice. Jonathan was in control. This wouldn't be their usual visit. Normally, they talked, kissed, and spent time together. As close as they'd come to sexual contact, they'd never crossed any real lines. Niall wasn't sure they could go back if they did.

He tore his mouth away. "Jonathan."

"No more talking," Jonathan spat as he fell to his knees. Niall reached for the man's arms, intent on pulling him back to his feet. Jonathan's hot mouth surrounded his cock, stealing Niall's ability to do anything at all. The sensitive nerve ending in his crown scraped the roof of Jonathan's mouth. The man's tongue lapped at every inch. Niall's fingers found Jonathan's soft hair and hung on.

It might've been his dream, but Niall knew he was no longer in charge. He wasn't sure how Jonathan controlled dreams or took control of certain aspects of people's minds, but there was no denying he belonged to Jonathan at the moment. Who was he kidding? Jonathan always owned him. The hot suction on his dick had Niall ready to tear his skin off. He needed his mate to make him come like he needed oxygen. Niall felt like he'd been dying for it for forever. Maybe it was all happening in his head, but Niall still wanted this his way. Using his unnatural strength against Jonathan, he swept his mate off his knees. After swiping everything off his worktable with his forearm, Niall set Jonathan on top. He tore at the man's clothes. He wasn't gentle. Niall didn't take it easy on him. The instant he had Jonathan unclothed enough to impale the man with his dick, he was inside his mate.

Jonathan scratched at his skin and pulled his hair. He writhed against Niall like he felt the same insanity Niall did—the same need to become one. Even once inside, Niall's inner rage didn't ease. This wasn't making love. It wasn't mating. Hell, Niall wasn't even sure it was sex. This was a branding. He wanted his mate's blood, sweat, and screams. His teeth tore into Jonathan's chest. Blood filled his mouth and ran down his chin. The copper scent was so strong, Niall swore it was really happening. The hot squeezing of his cock felt every bit as real. The fire in his gut exploded into waves of ecstasy, stealing everything from Niall—his cum. A scream. His soul.

Warm jets of semen filled his underwear, pulling him from the dream of Jonathan. A gasp tore from his throat as his eyes shot open. He blinked at the sight of his bedroom. The blank walls matched the emptiness of waking up to find Jonathan missing.

Niall glanced down at his soaked underwear. "Fook." The growled word echoed in the empty room, reminding Niall how alone he was in the world. Throwing his arm over his eyes, Niall shut out his surroundings and concentrated on breathing. This wouldn't kill him. His throat tightened. Pain sliced through him. His arms had never felt emptier. Then again, maybe this would kill him after all.

*

Jonathan didn't come to bed at dawn as promised. Cin tried to stop his rage from growing. Two hours past time for bed, Cin snapped. The sexy man who'd stolen Cin's heart had no fucking clue how hard Cin had to fight to keep his alpha side from demanding Jonathan give him everything. After searching the house, he headed for the garage. With every step, he prayed he wouldn't find Jonathan still hanging out with the demon spawn.

Before he could temper his reaction, Cin threw the door open with enough force it bounced off the wall and almost closed again.

The demon eyed him, looking bored by the show of rage. His gaze swept the room. Jonathan was asleep on a cot in the corner. It took every ounce of his willpower not to kill the spawn right then. It didn't matter the creature had nothing to do with Jonathan choosing the garage over the bed he shared with Cin. Someone should feel his wrath.

"Why the fook is he with you?" Cin asked before he could call the question back.

The demon snorted. It was an ugly sound. "You really don't want my opinion on that."

Cin knelt beside the cot and inspected Jonathan's sleeping form. He didn't think the demon could do Jonathan harm from his trap, but he wouldn't take any chances with his heart. "You're right. I don't," Cin said absently. Jonathan looked like an angel when he slept. His long eyelashes fanned across his cheeks. Cin had to stop himself from brushing his fingertip over them. Before Jonathan, he'd never loved a single soul beyond his clansmen. Everything was falling apart, and he was trying his ass off to hang on. He would die without this man. Cin couldn't understand why Jonathan didn't see him fading away.

When he couldn't stand it another second, Cin traced the curve of Jonathan's cheek. The man didn't stir.

"He's exhausted," the demon said, surprising Cin with the affection in his voice. As far as he knew, demons felt nothing.

"I know. He's still adjusting to the turn." Cin had no idea why he confessed as much.

The demon scoffed. "Whatever helps

you sleep at night."

Cin didn't bother arguing. Demons could smell lies like vampires smelled blood. Instead, he scooped Jonathan from the cot like he was a child. The man still didn't stir. Without a backward glance, Cin headed for bed. He wasn't sleeping without Jonathan at his side. After getting Jonathan tucked into bed, Cin stripped out of his clothes. A low knock landed on the door. Cin didn't bother covering up. He was too old for modesty, and there was no part of him that his clan hadn't seen. He found Niall standing on the other side of the door. The giant vamp looked like hell. He had dark circles under his eyes and his beard was getting out of control. A wave of loneliness overcame Cin. It took him a moment to realize the sensation came from Niall. His gaze skirted in every direction as if he couldn't meet Cin's stare.

"Is your offer to sleep here still open?"

Cin stepped aside in way of answer. Niall shuffled into the room as if still unsure of his welcome. He eyed Jonathan's sleeping form.

"I found him on a cot in the garage a few minutes ago. He's pretty out of it."

Niall finally met his gaze at the confession. His brow furrowed, showing his confusion. "Is he okay?"

Cin shrugged and moved to scoot Jonathan to the center of the bed. He climbed into his usual spot, leaving room for Niall to claim Jonathan's other side. The moment he was settled with Jonathan's heat resting against him and his prince's strength filling the room, Cin heard himself admitting his worst fears.

"I think we're all slowly dying without each other, and I'm out of ideas on how to fix it. You can't live without him. He can't live without you, and I won't survive without either of you. Please tell me what

I'm supposed to do?"

The silence hanging between them stretched on for so long Cin didn't think Niall would respond. "I'm the thief here. You gave away everything to stay and serve me, and now here we are."

"Yeah, well, don't forget your father locked me away. I'd rather serve a prince who loves me than a king who uses me."

Niall's hand found Cin's beneath the covers. "I do love you."

"Then trust me," Cin said, refusing to hold back.

"I do."

"Then be the badass warrior prince I left everything behind for, because I need you. Jonathan needs you. Someone has to be the one holding us together, and we're weaker apart."

"I'm trying."

Cin couldn't let up. "Try harder."

This time, Niall didn't bother

responding. It didn't matter. With the man's steady presence, clicking them together like a finished puzzle, Cin felt the weight on his shoulders slipping away.

Chapter 8

Niall needed to blow off steam. Jonathan had come to him in a dream and left Niall a mess. So much so, he'd ended up begging to be accepted into Cin's bed. After a night of holding his mate, he needed to run or hit something. He didn't care which, as long as it made his muscles scream. Niall almost made it out the door before Faolan called out, stopping him.

"You had all our things moved, right?"

Niall peeked inside the kitchen. Faolan had torn it apart. Pots and pans covered every surface. Every drawer and cabinet stood open. "Aye, you know I did," Niall said as he eyed the mess.

"What happened to that big frying pan thingie that we used to cook stir fry and whatnot?"

Niall couldn't claim Faolan hadn't looked. "Last I saw, it was in the big closet in the hall." Because that was their catchall. If they hadn't been able to find a place to put something, they'd used the huge closet in the hall that seemed to have no other purpose.

"I looked in there already."

In that case, the closet was now—most likely—every bit as big of a mess as the kitchen. "It's on the shelf."

"Looked on the shelf."

While swiping his hand over his face, Niall headed for the closet. If he didn't find the damn pan, Faol was likely to tear the whole house down around them. The instant he opened the door, Niall almost slammed it closed again. Jonathan and Cin were half-dressed, hair standing on end. They'd obviously found a quiet spot and were five seconds away from steaming up the place. Before Niall could pull the door closed, leaving them to it, a shove came from behind. The door slammed, shutting him inside with the aroused pair. He turned the knob, ready to make a run for it. Nothing happened.

"The door's locked." Niall wasn't surprised as much as he was confused.

"Yeah. I think that's part of the plan," Cin said. Laughter laced his words. "We've been stuck inside here for over an hour. Not that we've minded."

"You could dissipate to the other side, if you want out," Jonathan suggested

"Nope," Niall said, hearing the way his voice had gone dead, but incapable of stopping it. Reaching above his head, Niall pulled the string, killing the light in the closet. Ancient symbols flared to life in glow-in-the-dark paint. "It's a vampire trap."

Jonathan turned in a circle and eyed the walls. "Why would you have a vampire trap in your house?"

A growl rose in Niall's throat. "It's your house too, and I didn't have one until the fool in our merry lot painted one."

Jonathan met his gaze. His green irises glowed beautifully in the dark. "Why would Faolan do that?"

Before he could stop himself, Niall ran his hand down Jonathan's back. It was dark. They were standing too close. Jonathan's breath caught at the back of his throat at the contact. It sounded as loud as gunfire to Niall.

Cin reached around Jonathan and tugged Niall closer. Jonathan's scent overcame him. Damn, the man was a mixture of sex and a candy shop. Niall wanted to lick him all day.

"You still smell like last night's dream." He did. Niall didn't know why he said as much. It was a stupid thing to say, especially with Cin eyeing him and obviously waiting to see what Niall would do next.

"Kiss me." Jonathan's voice came out on a whisper, hardening Niall's cock.

Niall stopped breathing. "I can't."

"Kiss me," Jonathan repeated.

"You know I can't." His gaze moved between Cin and Jonathan. He swore both men held their breath—waiting. "If I kiss you, I won't stop," Niall admitted, because—apparently—he had zero control over his tongue today.

"Then promise me you won't move."

It was an odd request. "Why?"

"Because I asked it of you," Jonathan said. His voice had gone soft, luring Niall in.

Since Niall had already denied Jonathan once, he gave in to the strange demand. "I promise."

Jonathan moved closer. Niall held his breath. Their gazes never wavered as Jonathan leaned in. "If you won't kiss me, it's up to us to kiss you." The air stuttered from Niall's lungs as Jonathan's lips touched the corner of his mouth. His lips moved from the corner of Niall's mouth to his bottom lip. The instant he took Niall's lip between his teeth, something broke inside him. His arm snaked out, snagging Cin. After finding the back of Cin's head with his grip, he pulled the man in, forcing a three-way kiss upon them. There was a vise on his heart, squeezing the life from him. The moment his tongue entwined with his men's, the death grip loosened. He could breathe again for the first time since turning Jonathan. In a moment of clarity, he realized all his fears of harming Cin for touching Jonathan had been ridiculous. The three of them—they were connected inside where no one could see.

Jonathan's fingers shaped Niall's erection through his pants. Niall's muscles tensed. Somewhere along the line, it had become a habit to resist. He didn't have to any longer. These men—they were his.

"Shhh," Jonathan soothed as he pulled the string loose on Niall's workout pants. "You promised." He'd sworn he'd be still. No way could he keep his word, but he knew what Jonathan really wanted. He wanted Niall to stop running. That was one promise he would keep. "You don't have to do anything," Jonathan said, his lips brushing Niall's chest with every syllable. "Just don't push us away."

Niall didn't know if he should answer or keep trying to kiss Cin. This was something they hadn't done in years. It wasn't until Jonathan came into their lives that Niall realized no one kissed him any longer. One day, it just stopped. But in every dream Jonathan created for them, he always kissed Niall, making him long for contact he hadn't realized he'd lost. Once he'd known what was missing from his life, he couldn't stop craving the stroke of a strong tongue against his.

He found his back shoved against the wall. Jonathan's mouth covered his. The man's hand dipped inside his pants. Cin tugged at Jonathan's clothes while Jonathan boldly stroked Niall's cock.

I'm about to suck your dick.

Niall nearly came as Jonathan's words shoved into his mind. Jonathan wasn't finished.

I'm about to take you down my throat. I expect you to stand here and take it because I am your mate. You owe me your pleasure.

Goddamn. This was his mate. He equaled Niall in every way. Niall didn't resist as Jonathan pushed the workout pants down his hips. At some point, Jonathan had lost his shirt. Niall ripped his over his head because he needed to feel the man's skin against his. Without warning, Jonathan bent at the waist and took Niall down his throat. It was so much more of everything in reality than the dream world. The heat of Jonathan's mouth. The brush of his tongue. Niall already knew this encounter would be embarrassingly short, especially considering the erotic sight of Cin positioning his dick to push his way inside Jonathan. Their gazes met as Cin shoved his way inside. Jonathan made a strangled sound around Niall's dick that nearly brought Niall to his knees. Niall reached for Cin. Cin's fingers linked with his.

"My prince."

My friend.

Cin's lips parted on a pant as Niall projected his words. Niall tore his gaze away from the vamp's open pleasure. He needed to watch as his saliva-soaked dick sawed in and out of his mate's mouth. His body was on fire. Everything inside him gravitated toward Jonathan. He just wanted to be with his mate. Niall no longer cared about the circumstances. Nothing else mattered. If the gods felt it necessary to decree he share this man, then there was a good reason, and it didn't matter at all. His heart didn't give a fuck. Right now, his body wasn't too concerned either. Damn. Jonathan had talent. The man's throat worked Niall's cock. Every noise the man made screamed he loved what they did to him. Niall wanted more.

"Play with yourself, gorgeous," Niall demanded, needing to watch Jonathan bring himself to orgasm.

Jonathan fisted his dick and weakened Niall's knees. Pleasure curled his toes before climbing up his body and drawing his balls up tight. As his orgasm hit, the confession tore from this throat on a growl. "You're both *mine*." His vision went black as Jonathan came. The man's orgasm mixed with Cin's inside Niall's mind, stealing all the oxygen from the room. They went down in a heap of legs and arms, shaking from the power of their union. Niall half expected the walls to crack around them from the explosion.

*

Jonathan lost track of time as he sat facing his men. Cin and Niall sat side by side, both eyeing him in hunger. It took every ounce of his willpower not to press his hand to his stomach to quell the butterflies.

"Eventually, we'll get out of this closet. When we do, I plan to do some dirty shit to both of you. Seriously, you'll wonder if you know me at all." The smiles stretching both men's lips had Jonathan taking a deep breath. He wanted everything, and he needed it now.

"I had another mate once," Niall said, stabbing Jonathan through the heart. His throat tightened and his eyes stung. It felt like a betrayal, not to mention blindsided. He was feeling a lot of that too at the moment. Jonathan had no clue where that tidbit had come from.

Cin's gaze flashed with fire as he glanced Niall's way. "Niall, you don't have to do this."

Niall's smile turned sad. "Aye. I do."

Jonathan was leaning toward agreeing with Cin. He didn't want to hear about another mate. Niall was his. Unfortunately, it seemed Niall was dead set on going there.

"He died. Starved to death, actually." Jonathan's insides clenched at the confession. He couldn't look away from Niall. "You've been so unhappy since the turn, I've half expected you'd do the same thing. Put me through the same hell. That's one of the reasons I've been scared to get too close."

Jonathan couldn't lie and say he

hadn't considered it. For months, he'd been tearing Cin and Niall apart while ripping himself to shreds in hopes of being everything to everyone. Dying had seemed the best for everyone.

A derisive-sounding snort filled the tiny space. Too late, Jonathan realized he hadn't been guarding his thoughts. Niall shook his head while holding Jonathan's stare. "You're so fucking blind, Jonathan. I'm near to being seven hundred years old. Cin is just over six. Haven't you stopped to think maybe we knew? We went into this thing fully aware of what would happen if I turned you." Niall ran both hands through his hair, leaving it standing on end. Jonathan could feel Niall's fury rising. Even Cin looked wary. "Fuck you," Niall spat, taking him by surprise with his anger. "Never once have I asked you to choose. Every day, I wake up and take a sledgehammer to my heart—for you. How dare you steal the only piece I have of you—the knowledge that you live? That you're somewhere in the world, breathing. I'd rather you take my life than leave me behind."

The idea of anything ever happening to Niall flashed through Jonathan's mind, threatening to rip his lungs out. For a moment, he swore he felt the flames of hell licking at his skin, letting him know how every day would be without Niall. He moved without thinking. He couldn't let Niall continue believing he would ever leave them. Jonathan pressed his forehead to Niall's while pulling Cin in as well. The three of them sat, eyes closed and breathing one another's air.

"How could you think you only have that piece of me?" Without giving Niall time to answer, he made a different demand he wasn't sure he could handle. "Tell me about this other mate and have it out there. We've spent too much time not talking to one another."

Cin was the first to speak as if he too felt Niall's inability to tell the tale. "It's not a pretty story."

Jonathan nodded. Dying rarely was attractive. "He starved to death," Jonathan said, getting the man started.

"There was a bit more to it than that," Cin said, obviously incapable of keeping the bitterness from his voice while Niall kept his eyes closed, as if he couldn't look at Jonathan while Cin spoke of a past he'd rather forget. "You see, in vampire society, it's considered unnatural for men to prefer men. I know there are humans who believe the same, but it's even more so in our world than the one you were born into, because we are all old," Cin said with a snort of laughter. There was no humor in the sound. "There are verra few vampires under the age of two hundred, and most of the elders believe being gay is a perversion brought on by age, rather than a way we are born."

Cin leaned back against the wall and stared into space as if remembering a time he couldn't forget. "Niall fell in love with a human back when we were all living in the same stronghold alongside our king. He turned the man in secret. Only Dougal, Faolan, and I knew. We'd sworn, if anything happened to Niall, we would make sure the man didn't starve."

Jonathan felt Niall take a deep breath. He smoothed his hand up Niall's thigh while hanging on Cin's every word, even though every one was like a dagger to his heart. It was hard as hell, hearing about his mate loving someone else, especially when he didn't think Niall loved him.

Niall's eyes opened. His gaze held Jonathan's, making Jonathan wonder if he'd heard his thoughts or if Niall needed to see Jonathan's reaction to the tale.

Cin kept talking as if oblivious to everything but the past. "Niall might be fourth in line for the throne with zero chance of ever sitting on it, but he's still a prince. His union was—for many reasons—considered an abomination. When his father learned of the man's existence, he had Niall imprisoned, and he tortured Niall's mate, Baodan, until he gave up our names as the ones keeping him fed."

"Oh my god." Jonathan couldn't stop the words from escaping. What a horrible bastard. King or not, Jonathan wanted to hunt the man down and make him pay.

Cin nodded. "He is an evil bastard. Anyhow, the three of us were thrown into a cell alongside Niall until Baodan passed to the next life. Once we were set free, we left, and haven't returned home since."

A sick feeling rose inside Jonathan. What would happen when the king learned Niall had a new mate? Would the same thing happen to him? For all he felt trapped here, he wasn't. He couldn't imagine being imprisoned or starving to death. That was a horrible way to die.

"Where does that leave me?" To his surprise, Jonathan's tone didn't hold an ounce of the fear that lived in his mind.

"You have nothing to worry about," Niall growled. "Times have changed a lot in our world. We've grown alongside the humans in our beliefs." His mate's face hardened, stirring butterflies in Jonathan's stomach once more. "And I

192

would kill anyone who thought to harm you."

Jonathan shook his head. "Sometimes, I feel very lost in this world I know nothing about. Everything has been flipped upside down since my turning, I hadn't stopped to consider if I could one day find myself as just one of many mates or god... I don't know—tossed aside when you get tired of this constant drama. I just..." Jonathan's hands rose for a moment before falling back to his lap, showing he had nothing. Things had been so crazy and internal, they'd avoided talking about anything of any importance. They skated around every heavy topic as if expecting it to blow up in their faces. He was exhausted from the strain.

"We bond for life," Cin said, as if attempting to set Jonathan's mind at ease.

Niall nodded. "It's chemical. Vampires

rarely have sex with other vampires, because the blood exchange, bonding them forever, can happen so easily once you get carried away. That's the biggest reason we turn to humans for blood and sex. Humans don't drink from us, so the commitment isn't there. Once a vampire is mated, the chemical in their blood that creates the bond is diluted, so there isn't enough of the hormone left in our systems to bond with anyone else. If your mate passes, your body will start producing more of the hormones needed. It's nature's way of keeping a pure blood line alive. Obviously, any one of us could still sleep with someone else, but the experience would be an extremely watered down version of what we have, so why bother? I'll never feel for anyone what I feel for you."

Jonathan's eyes brows pulled

together. He felt it happen. "But I don't feel less for Cin because I feel..." Jonathan stopped before he said all the things running through his head. He didn't feel less for Cin because he loved Niall. Because he could feel a connection so deep with Niall, he thought he'd drown. No matter what words he chose, they all sounded like he belonged to Niall and only Niall. In Jonathan's heart, he couldn't accept that.

Cin flashed him a sad smile. "It's okay."

Jonathan shook his head. "It's not." His chest expanded as he drew the breath needed to confess the one thing that had been tearing his soul to shreds. Everyone deserved the truth. "Because I love you both. It's not fair—to either of you, but it's there, sitting on my chest all the time. I've tried to stop loving both of you." Jonathan rubbed the center of his chest as he said the words. Even the admission hurt. "But I can't." Pain overcame Jonathan. He couldn't meet Cin or Niall's gaze. Instead he chose to stare at his hands. "And I know, one of these days, you'll find your mate and then I'll be a distant memory." He finally met Cin's stare. "If I lose you today or five hundred years from now, it'll hurt me just as much. I know I need to set you free and let you find your other half, because I belong to Niall. Help me let you go."

Cin snorted. His smile took Jonathan by surprise. "Niall is right. You are *so* blind. Have I bored you since you turned? Am I less in your eyes?"

Jonathan shook his head. It was true. He'd been all over the man since the turn. "If anything, we've been more intense."

"For fook's sake," Niall growled,

making Cin jump, as if he'd forgotten the man's presence. "Cin is your mate too," Niall said, as if he couldn't take another second of listening to Cin beat around the bush. "That's why this shit's been so hard on everyone. If I was your only choice, Cin would've been out of the picture no matter what you felt for him before the turn. You can't fight a mating. It's stronger than anything you knew as a human."

Jonathan's gaze moved between them. Instead of relief, Jonathan was disheartened. This was another thing he didn't understand. "How is that possible?"

Cin shrugged. "We'd both taken your blood shortly before you turned and you ingested both of ours during your turning. Actually, all three of our bloods mixed in the process of trying to save you." Cin shook his head. "I'm sure we're not the first case of this happening, but it's rare."

"So, no matter what happens, we'll all end up miserable. That's fucking fantastic," Jonathan said, feeling worse by the second. "You really should've let me die, after all."

A sexy smile twisted Cin's lips. "Come here, baby," Cin said, holding his hand out for Jonathan. Despite Jonathan's fears and earlier request for Cin to let him go, Jonathan immediately accepted. As soon as Jonathan settled between Niall and Cin, Cin squashed the man between them, doing a damn good job of holding Jonathan and Niall.

"Can everyone just be still for a little while?" Cin asked, incapable of hiding the hope everyone would listen for once. Niall scooched closer and joined Cin in holding Jonathan. "I feel like I'm the only one who realizes we're all trying so hard to make each other happy that we're making each other miserable. Why is that?"

"I don't want to hurt anyone," Jonathan answered, willing to talk things out. "But I also can't help how I feel."

Niall pressed a light kiss to Jonathan's ear. "I love both of you too much to hurt you."

Cin didn't look surprised by Niall's confession.

Jonathan was over the moon. "Awwww," Jonathan said. "You said you loved me."

A dimple appeared in Niall's cheek. "Idiot." Niall said the word with so much affection it sounded more like an endearment than an insult.

Cin shifted so he could hold Jonathan's gaze. "Are you paying attention? Niall just told you he loves you with me sitting right here. Do I look angry?"

Jonathan shook his head. He didn't, and Jonathan didn't know what to do with that.

"That's because it's okay for him to love you and you're allowed to love him back," Cin said, sounding as if it should've been obvious. "You're blood mates. That's huge in our world. The three of us, we're connected in a way few people ever get to experience. It's overwhelming, but also sort of amazing. You have such a human view on things. I know it's hard for you to understand, but when you've lived for hundreds of years, things aren't as black and white." His smile turned wicked. "And there's verra little we haven't done thousands of times."

Jonathan pinched him. He couldn't help it. No one wanted to hear shit like that from their mate. Cin laughed and rubbed the spot where Jonathan got him. His expression turned serious. "If anything happened to you, it would kill me."

"Aye," Niall said. "Me too."

Jonathan's hand shot to his stomach. Their words hit home. "I have so much to lose," Jonathan said, barely whispering the words.

"Aye," Cin said. "We all do. But we're also luckier than most mates. When I need to go into battle or Niall does, we know one of us will always be with you. Eternity is long, Jonathan."

"So fucking long," Niall said, pressing Cin's point.

"We have each other."

"Aye," Niall said, having Cin's back.

"The heart doesn't care what the mind thinks. Can we please stop trying to force our hearts into doing our minds' bidding?" Cin asked with desperation lacing the question. "I love you both. I'm begging for it to be enough, because I can't fight both of you and a pack of demons."

Jonathan smiled at the affection in Cin's voice. All three of them had admitted their love, and there had been no ugliness or jealousy, as Jonathan had feared. With the knowledge they'd be fine settled firmly in his mind, other thoughts sneaked in. He had two gorgeous alpha men. Jonathan took a deep breath, trying to squelch his growing desire. He could do so many things—dirty things.

"How long do you think Faolan will leave us locked in here?"

Niall's low chuckle rolled over Jonathan's skin, making his dick stir. "If I know him, he's probably listening at the door and stroking his cock."

"I resent that," Faolan said, his voice muffled by the wood separating them.

Jonathan's body shook with laughter. "How did this happen to me and what the hell am I supposed to do with a band of misfit Scots?"

"Just throwing this out there," Faolan said through the door. "But I vote for an orgy."

"Oh, God."

"It's Goddess Celeste, actually," Faolan said, obviously intent on hanging out.

Jonathan took turns eyeing Niall and Cin. "If I ask, will he go away, let us out, or ask to join?"

The door flew open. "Join?"

Jonathan couldn't stop laughing. Not

only did he feel lighter than he had in ages, he'd never been more thankful they were all—for the most part—dressed.

Chapter 9

This time, Jonathan was the one who couldn't stop pacing. He could feel Lire's stare upon him like heat blasting his skin. Time grew short. They stood on the edge of something. Jonathan wanted to talk about it, but he didn't know where to start. It wasn't as if he could explain the sensation in his gut. Something was coming. Once, when he was eight, he'd broken his leg while out hiking with his dad. For years afterward, his leg would ache, letting him know when it was about to rain. This was the same, except it was Jonathan's whole body and he didn't know what was coming. All he knew was—now was the time to settle this. Lire needed to tell him what he could, and Jonathan had to find a way to save him.

"Ask me about last night before it

drives you insane," Lire said, as if he couldn't take the silence any longer.

Jonathan shook his head. "You don't have to explain. I researched Lilin-demons. Just as I need blood to survive, you need sex. Of course, someone has to feed you."

Lire released a derisive-sounding snort. "Starvation is a common torture method. So, no. No one has to do anything."

At Lire's words, Jonathan stopped pacing and met his gaze. "I didn't mean to insult you. By the looks of things, he wasn't here by duty or obligation."

"That's not—" Lire began.

Jonathan shook his head, cutting him off. "Don't lie to me, okay. It's obvious you can read my mind. You know I can tell when you lie. I don't expect you to tell me anything you don't want to." It hit Jonathan. Lire hadn't considered lying to him before today. What if he asked? Point blank asked Lire where to find the pack?

Lire shook his head and pressed his finger to his lips. "You have a guard."

Jonathan's eyebrows rose. "Do I?"

"A sentry," Lire said with a nod.

Ah. Someone listened at the door. "I forgot something," Jonathan said, heading for the door. He opened it and nearly tripped over Faolan. He stepped out and snapped the door closed behind him before Faolan got any ideas about heading inside.

"Did Niall talk to you about how I'll be the only one questioning our guest?"

Faolan didn't appear the least bit guilty. "Aye."

"Okay," Jonathan said, dragging out the word. "Then what's up?"

"He didn't tell me to stay away. Just no torture. You need someone watching your back. Despite the reason for your turn, you have no idea what you're dealing with."

Jonathan cast a glance around, trying to decide what to do. He didn't want to alienate his clansman, but neither could he let this go on. "What if I told you not to do this?"

A sweet smile touched Faolan's lips, making Jonathan feel twice as guilty. "Then I've had one prince tell me I'm not allowed to torture this demon, and one prince tell me he doesn't want me guarding him. I'm not sure if I'll follow either order, since I like being spanked. You know, for future reference," he added with a wink.

"That's good to kno—" Jonathan stopped mid-sentence as the full impact of Faolan's words hit. "Did you just call me your prince?"

"Aye. That's how it works."

This life made Jonathan feel like he was always slow catching on. "Huh. Guess it hadn't occurred to me. Anyhow," Jonathan said, putting that detail in a box for later and moving on, "as thrilling as I'm sure hanging outside this door is, I need you to check out something else for me."

"Anything, my prince," Faolan said with a short bow.

Jonathan pinched the spot between his eyes where pain bloomed. "Is this going to be a new thing? Because I don't like it."

Faolan's smile was unrepentant. "I know."

A loud sigh escaped Jonathan before he could call it back. "Moving on. Can you check out pier thirty-seven in Port Andrew? I've been looking at maps, and I think that's the one."

The giant vamp's smile fell. He took Jonathan's hand between his. "Look, Jonathan. I know you think you know what you're doing in there, but this demon isn't your friend, and he isn't..." Pain bloomed behind Jonathan's left eye. His vision blurred. Faolan was still talking. Jonathan couldn't hear a word. Everything inside him went dark—like his mind grasped to accept the emptiness inside Faolan. He couldn't breathe around the pain beneath Faolan's smile. A chill raced down his spine. Goosebumps rose on his skin. Faolan's lips were moving. No sound could penetrate the void.

"The demon says you have no heart,"

Jonathan said before he could stop himself.

Faolan squeezed his hand once more before letting him go. The instant Faolan released him, the world snapped back into focus. Air rushed back into his lungs. Faolan looked sad. "I didn't think. You don't have to worry about me touching you again. I'll go check out your pier."

Before Faolan could get away, Jonathan stepped into his path and set his hands on Faolan's chest. This time, he knew what to expect, and the impact wasn't as severe. He took a deep breath to steady himself before attempting to speak. "Don't stop trying. See," he said, nodding toward his hands. "You can touch me. I won't break. Don't stop trying," he repeated, because it was important, and skin on skin contact was the only thing that would ever heal Faolan.

Faolan set his hands over Jonathan's, holding him in place. A smirk touched his lips. Wicked intent lit his amethyst eyes. "I'll touch you as much you'd like, my prince. Just let me know when and where."

With a roll of his eyes, Jonathan took a step back. "Let me know what you find at the pier. I feel it in my gut. That's the one they used."

Faolan's playful smile slipped away. His gaze sharpened. "Used?"

Jonathan gave him a sharp nod. "I think we're in the wrong place, but I can't prove it. Go check out the pier and leave me in peace so I can find out the truth."

This time when Faolan gave him a short bow, he meant it. Jonathan let it slide since he didn't think he could make Faolan stop. He waited until Faolan was gone before searching the garage for what he needed. After grabbing a can of white paint and a brush, he slipped back inside with Lire. With the door closed, shutting them away, Jonathan locked it. If any of his clansmen wanted inside, a locked door wouldn't slow them, but it would give Jonathan a half second of warning. He started with the symbol painted on the back door. With a small brush stroke, he transformed the symbol for a demon trap into a demon ward, making the room impenetrable.

When Lire realized what Jonathan had done, he came to his feet. Jonathan moved to the next set of markings. He didn't know how he knew what to draw, but he did. The ancient symbols lived in his head. Once he'd changed all the symbols on the walls, he moved to the center of the room and held Lire's stare.

"If I ask where your pack is, will you answer?"

"Yes."

Jonathan gave a sharp nod at the honesty in Lire's answer. "Why?"

Lire lifted one shoulder in a half shrug. "I'm dead already. The enemy of my enemy, as they say."

"You're not dead," Jonathan said. His gaze never wavered. "At least, not yet. I may not be able to save you from my clansmen, but I can give you a fighting chance and I can protect you from what's coming."

Lire's expression shifted. It was a subtle hint of surprise, quickly masked, but it was enough. Lire knew it too—evil headed their way.

"You know what's coming," Jonathan

accused.

Lire held his stare. "You should leave here, Jonathan."

"Where's your pack, Lire?"

"You already know."

"I know where they aren't," Jonathan shot back every bit as quickly.

Lire's mouth lifted in one corner. "Then you know where they are."

It was as he thought. Lire wasn't part of the pack. Jonathan didn't know why the demon had been there the day his throat had been slit, but it wasn't because he was part of the pack they'd been hunting.

"Where is the pack we've been hunting?"

Lire's smile turned wicked. "Now that's the million-dollar question, isn't it? You're a lesson ahead of your friends who've lived hundreds of years longer. If you want a straight answer from a demon, ask the right question. There's a pack of demons using a set of seven ships and several smaller crafts safely keeping to the waters, unless supplies are needed." Such as women. Those poor women. "Your friends could search for the rest of eternity and never find them."

"Why?"

Lire flattened his hands against his invisible cage, looking like a mime. "For the same reason I can't leave this circle."

It was so simple. So fucking simple, he couldn't believe no one had considered it. Just as they'd trapped Lire with magic, the demons had done the same to create an impenetrable stronghold in the one place no one would stumble across them. Mark their ships with magic symbols and sail around the world completely invisible from detection—genius.

"Where are they?"

Lire shook his head. "You're the only one who knows."

"Me? How am I supposed to know?" Jonathan asked, almost desperate for answers now.

"That's not the right question, Jonathan."

With a growl, Jonathan gave up. He needed to finish his task before another of the men came looking to guard him. After dropping to his haunches, Jonathan changed the symbol on the floor. With that half of the trap transformed, he grabbed the chair and climbed on. He quickly swiped an extra line on the ceiling, breaking the trap and completely protecting Lire from evil. The instant Lire was free, his arms encircled Jonathan's waist. He lifted Jonathan from the chair and set Jonathan on his feet, making sure their bodies brushed from hip to sternum in the process. Jonathan tried not to let it affect his breathing.

Lire's palm touched Jonathan's jaw. He held Jonathan in place. Their gazes never wavered. "I can't decide if you're the biggest fool to ever walk the planet or if I should kiss you and make you mine."

"You could kiss me, but I'll never be yours."

Lire brushed his fingertips along Jonathan's bottom lip. "Ah, yes. Your prince and warrior."

"No," Jonathan said with a smile, feeling dazed, and not at all immune to Lire's spell. "Your Dougal."

A smile exploded across Lire's face. "Dougal. So that's Blondy's name." He said

Dougal's name with such lust, Jonathan almost didn't regret giving him the vamp's name. Almost.

"At least I now know how I'll die. Dougal's going to kill me."

Lire shook his head. "It'll be our secret."

Jonathan couldn't help but wonder if he was trusting Lire with too many secrets. At what point would this demon own his soul?

*

Niall waited in the shadows, biding his time. All he knew was hunger. He'd gotten a taste of his mate. Now he needed more. It was an obsession, eating at the back of his mind. Jonathan came through the door. His forehead furrowed as he mulled over something deep. The man was damn sexy. Niall stayed still, holding out until

Jonathan closed the bedroom door behind him before attacking. His form shimmered as he slipped quietly from one point to the space at Jonathan's back. His arms automatically sought Jonathan's waist. He pulled his gorgeous mate back against his chest. Jonathan melted. His body molded with Niall's.

"Niall." Jonathan's whisper sounded like a benediction.

"Need you," Niall growled against Jonathan's nape. His hands traveled south. His mouth opened over the cords of Jonathan's neck.

"Niall," Jonathan repeated. "I love you."

Niall froze at the admission. It hit him in the chest. He turned Jonathan in his arms. Jonathan's expression had Niall sucking in an audible breath. The man's heart was in his eyes. Niall leaned in, moving slowly. He wanted to savor the moment. Their lips met. For half a second, Jonathan held Niall's bottom lip between his teeth before their kiss exploded. It was everything a mate's kiss should be—hot and beyond compare. This was the reason he could never turn elsewhere. Jonathan's kiss kept Niall so enthralled he didn't realize Jonathan had him half undressed until Jonathan palmed his erection. Niall grabbed two handfuls of ass and lifted Jonathan off the ground while still eating at the man's mouth. When he finally thought he might be able to stand giving up Jonathan's kiss, he tossed the man onto the bed.

Jonathan's chest rose and fell as he struggled for air. Niall held the man's gaze as he stripped. Once nude, he peeled off Jonathan's clothes as well. He stole as many caresses as he could. When not a stitch of clothing stood between them,

Niall covered Jonathan's body with his.

"I love you, Jonathan. I love you," he repeated as he claimed the man's mouth. He changed angles. "I'm so in love with you."

Jonathan's hold tightened. "Then take away this ache. You're the missing piece."

At Jonathan's plea, Niall pushed from the bed and searched the room. He found a bottle of lube and moved back to stand over Jonathan. "You're mine."

"I am," Jonathan said, sounding breathless in his agreement.

"There's no going back from here," Niall warned. "You'll crave me all the time."

"That's already true."

Jonathan's claim sucker-punched Niall in the gut. His mate's expression— like desire and madness — had Niall rushing through lubing up. Jonathan watched him through hooded eyes. Niall savored the slick pressure of stroking his oiled cock while tormenting his mate.

Jonathan wasn't one to wait for any man. In one smooth motion, he sat, towed Niall into bed, and straddled Niall's hips. Gorgeous green eyes stared down at him as Jonathan took Niall inside. Niall held his breath as Jonathan's greedy ass pulled him deep. It had finally happened. He'd claimed his mate, or Jonathan had claimed him. It didn't matter. They were one. There was no better sensation than Jonathan's ass squeezing him. They'd just gotten started and Niall felt like they'd been edging for hours. His skin burned. He was desperate for orgasm but more so for Jonathan's. Niall wanted to watch and feel as Jonathan came unglued.

Jonathan's teeth sank into Niall's chest. His tongue had Niall's skin tingling. "Damn, Niall," Jonathan gasped as he sat back and rocked himself on Niall's dick.

With his head thrown back and stroking his cock while riding Niall's, Jonathan was the picture of sexiness. Niall couldn't as much as blink. He didn't want to miss a thing. Jonathan's chin dropped to his chest. His eyes opened. Niall sucked in a gasp at the lust staring at him. He came. The orgasm slammed into him without warning. His muscles seized. Jonathan's name ripped from his throat. Jonathan fell forward and captured Niall's mouth, as if he needed to taste his name on Niall's tongue. Hot cum filled the space between them. Jonathan's ass squeezed Niall's dick with the same rhythm of the jets of semen hitting Niall's chest.

Jonathan's ragged breaths brushed Niall's ear as Jonathan trailed kisses from the corner of Niall's mouth to his ear. The man's tongue tickled the shell.

"Our souls met," Jonathan said as he nipped at Niall's lobe. It was true. Niall was too blown away to respond. Jonathan sucked on his ear for a second before saying anything else. The next time he spoke, Niall wondered if he'd ever go soft again. "I wanted it sweet our first time. Next time, it'll be twisted. Scratches on your back. Handprints on my ass. Blood on the sheets. My name on your lips."

Niall held Jonathan tight against his chest. It was the only response he had in the face of the fire burning in his gut. Niall knew, even if it was possible for him to get bored with his mate, Jonathan would never let it happen.

Chapter 10

There was nothing worse than being wet while wearing clothes. Cin's feet squished inside his boots. If he was a human, he'd have been dead from pneumonia already. Jonathan had a lead on a certain port. Or a hunch. Whatever. He trusted Jonathan's gut feeling above all else. After Faolan had spent the day staking out the place, he'd agreed with Jonathan's assessment. Although he hadn't seen anything to back up Jonathan's gut feeling, the location was a solid place. They could load just about anything onto a boat without anyone seeing them. It was secluded, but close enough to a few popular nightclubs for the demons to lure unsuspecting women to their deaths. Just like in Tortola.

Cin and Faolan spent most of the night hiding in the trees, hoping to spot something of use. When the rain started falling, they'd buckled down, but when the lightning and thunder rolled in, they'd packed it in for the night. Now Cin was soaked to the bone, his mood was shit, and all he wanted was to crawl into bed with his men. He almost made it to the bedroom before an arm snaked out, towing him inside Niall's room. His chest hit a solid wall named Niall. Damn, he'd forgotten. He'd forgotten what it was like to have a warrior prince unleashing lust upon him.

"You're wet."

Cin held Niall's gaze and nodded. Anything he said would sound idiotic since Niall already pointed out the obvious.

Niall's gaze dropped to Cin's mouth. "We missed you today."

Cin's tongue shot out, wetting his

bottom lip. "Is that so?" Cin heard the lust dripping from his question.

"Yes. We should find Jonathan and coax him to bed. Get you warmed up."

Cin's heart sped. All hint of cold slipped away. His skin was on fire. This was what he'd been craving, having Niall take away the control. When Cin responded, his voice came out sounding like he'd been chomping on gravel. "Agreed." He took a step back, intent on doing just that.

Niall held tight, refusing to let him go. "In a second. We have business first." Cin was on the verge of panting from listening to Niall talk.

Cin nodded. His voice gone. Niall dipped his chin. Cin held his breath. When their lips met, a whimper escaped Cin. Niall's tongue swept Cin's bottom lip, seeking entrance. Cin's lips parted on a gasp. Niall took advantage, shoving his way inside. Without thought, Cin's fingers grasped at Niall's shirt, seeking purchase. His head fell back as Niall came at him with everything he had. It was a full-on assault. He was mindless, moving against Niall, seeking relief.

A noise like the tiniest shifting of weight had them jumping apart and spinning toward the door. Dougal stood with a spoon raised halfway to his mouth, a bowl in his other hand, and a look of shock etching his features. He cleared his throat and dropped the spoon into his bowl.

"Um, so, not judging here or anything, but is this the reason Jonathan is standing outside in the storm and looking scary? I tried reading him, even though I know he doesn't like that, but it was...

odd. There was nothing. Like a blank spot where he stood. It was fooking eerie."

Niall's face screwed up in confusion. He met Cin's gaze. "I can't hear him. He's hiding."

Cin gave him a shove toward the door. "You should be the one to go after him. If he's shielding his thoughts, I'll never break through."

Niall eyed him for a moment. "We should go together."

He was right. They should. Cin flashed his prince a smile. They were getting there—learning how to be a team. As a unit, they went in search of Jonathan. Dougal was right. Whatever was going on with Jonathan was eerie as hell. With his eyes closed, Jonathan stood out in the storm. His forehead furrowed as if lost in thought or concentrating with everything he possessed.

Cin brushed his fingertips down Jonathan's spine. "Hey, baby. Is everything okay?"

Jonathan didn't budge. He didn't startle at their appearance. If Cin wasn't mistaken, not a single muscle shifted. "Something's wrong."

Niall pulled a knife from its holster at his back at Jonathan's warning. Cin felt it then. Evil tainted the air. The storm dampened the scent of rot.

"Get inside, Jonathan," Niall ordered, attempting to shove Jonathan toward the house.

Jonathan didn't waver, even with the giant vamp trying to maneuver him. "I can't move."

Too late, Cin realized Jonathan wasn't

deep in thought. He was fighting the hold of some invisible evil that was keeping his body locked in place. Thankfully, Cin was still packing from his stakeout. Even as he pulled a gun and a knife from their holsters, his fangs grew, anticipating a fight. His senses strained, attempting to pinpoint from which direction they'd be attacked first.

Two demons dropped from the trees and rushed them from the left. Jonathan threw back his head, releasing a roar that startled Cin to the point he almost let one of their intruders get the drop on him. Not only did Jonathan's rage break through the invisible bonds holding him, his yell had Dougal and Faolan running full speed into battle as more demons poured in from every direction. Cin's attention was split between killing as many demons as possible and keeping Jonathan safe. This was why he'd wanted Jonathan to stay as far away from what they did as possible. He needed to know his man was safe.

Cin need not have worried. The one demon who managed to break through the barrier of warriors surrounding Jonathan paid for his efforts. Everyone froze as Jonathan's fingers wrapped around the demon's throat. He lifted the beast off its feet. The show of strength had nothing to do with the scattering demons, disappearing into the same trees they emerged from. The unlucky beast who suffered Jonathan's wrath shook with such a force the human he possessed slipped to the ground, leaving the demon behind in Jonathan's hold. Cin couldn't look away from the phenomenon. Outside of exorcism, Cin had never seen a demon ripped from human form by sheer power.

"There's nothing here for you,"

Jonathan growled, sounding like five deep-voiced men spoke from his mouth. A hint of fear snaked its way into Cin's heart. Jonathan was more than they believed, but what... he had no idea. With a squeeze of his fingers, Jonathan crushed the life from the demon before tossing him aside. Cin could only stare in disbelief. Jonathan hadn't sent the beast back to hell until he could find a new human to possess. He'd ended its existence.

The air turned to ice. Chills skirted over Cin. It had been centuries since Cin had felt such concentrated evil. He knew before turning his head what he would see. The grass died beneath the man's feet as he moved in their direction. His iridescent eyes were fixed upon Jonathan. The man's pale skin and perfect suit looked like a thousand other businessmen's. It was wrapping, masking one of the oldest evils of time — one of the original seven. Mammon. The only Prince of Hell incapable of sharing earth.

Cin moved to position himself between Mammon and Jonathan. Mammon's form turned to static. One second, he was feet away. The next, his fist slammed into Jonathan's chest. Blood splattered across Cin's face. His heart stopped. He could not do this twice in one lifetime. Losing Jonathan wasn't an option. A roar rent the air. Cin thought the sound came from his heart until he realized it was a mixture of the clan. Every single one released a battle cry as they launched themselves in Mammon's direction. Jonathan came to his own rescue. It was obvious Mammon intended to rip out Jonathan's heart, ensuring they couldn't save him. Jonathan shoved, sending Mammon sprawling. If the demon was surprised to find himself on the ground and under attack from a new turn, Cin didn't get a chance to enjoy the sight. The static zapping happened again, flashing the man away. Jonathan fell forward, landing in the mud. Faolan and Dougal took off after Mammon, leaving Cin and Niall scrambling to inspect Jonathan's injuries. Considering the fury with which Jonathan had fought for his life, Cin couldn't believe the massive hole in Jonathan's chest. It was healing, but not fast enough. Jonathan was losing blood faster than a gaping hole could close.

"Stay with me, baby," Niall begged, stealing the words from Cin's mouth.

"Lire," Jonathan whispered.

Niall cast a desperate glance at Cin. He bent closer, obviously trying to make sense of Jonathan's request. "I don't understand, baby. Just be still."

"Get Lire," Jonathan repeated.

The instant the request left Jonathan's lips, Niall disappeared in a flash of white light and smoke, as if he'd been zapped away. Cin found his back against a nearby tree. His feet hung feet off the ground. Nothing held him in place, except everything did. The world pressed against his chest, making it almost impossible for him to draw in enough air to breathe. Cin couldn't move. His voice wouldn't work. Niall had disappeared as if he never existed. Cin was rendered useless.

The demon they'd kept locked away appeared in the spot where Niall had been stooped at Jonathan's side, as if he could've overtaken them anytime he wanted. "I'm here," he said. The demon didn't hesitate digging his knees in the mud as he dropped to Jonathan's side and inspected the man's wounds.

"Get away from him." Cin mouthed the

words in a silent scream. Panic owned him. Jonathan was hurt and helpless against the creature currently kneeling over his body.

The demon never spared a glance for Cin. "Don't worry over your dark prince," he said, as if attempting to soothe Jonathan. "He's safe."

"I know," Jonathan gasped. He clung to the demon's hand, showing a trust in evil that infuriated Cin almost as much as his impotency did. "I can feel him."

"You should've run when I told you to, Jonathan," the demon said, seeming oblivious to the carnage surrounding him. "Your dark prince should've protected you. You're too important."

This dark creature knew Jonathan's name. Spoke as if they were friends. Cin was trapped. His mate's life was fading.

Niall was gone, and Cin didn't for a second trust a demon's words that his prince was safe. He'd never felt more powerless.

We've lost track of the evil one.

Dougal's mental update had Cin calling out for help in the only way left to him.

The demon has Jonathan.

Dougal and Faolan instantly appeared at his mental call. Unfortunately, they were as helpless as Cin the moment they showed themselves.

"What the fook?" Dougal yelled. Cin released a silent growl over Dougal having a voice. "Where's Niall?"

The demon flashed him away. I don't know where.

"I can heal you, Jonathan, but using dark magic this strong requires a trade."

"You son-of-a-bitch," Dougal yelled.

The demon continued to ignore him. "It has to be a life for a life. You're too close to death's edge. You can't cheat a reaper from gathering his allotted souls."

Jonathan shook his head. His teeth chattered as he spoke, as if the chill of death was upon him. "It's okay. I'm not scared."

"I cannot let you die, Jonathan."

"Yes you can," Jonathan gasped out, still clinging to the demon.

"Take me," Dougal cried out, sounding as if he was as desperate as Cin. "Save my prince. A life for a life. Take mine."

The demon finally tore his gaze away from Jonathan. His stare glowed red as it locked on Dougal. "I'd always intended on it, my love." The creature's hands glowed with unnatural light. He pushed the light into Jonathan's wound, tearing a scream from Jonathan that ripped at Cin's throat. Helpless tears of frustration rolled down Cin's cheeks. The demon spoke quietly to Jonathan. Cin couldn't hear a word over his mate's screams. Jonathan's body went still—lifeless.

Cin strained to hear any sound. A low pulse reached his ears. It was slow at first before gathering strength. It was his mate's heart beating. The demon and Dougal disappeared in the same flash of light as Niall had. Faolan's and Cin's bodies fell to the ground in a graceless heap. Cin scrambled to Jonathan's side. The wound in his chest was completely healed, but he didn't regain consciousness. There were too many things that he needed to do—find the evil responsible. Search for Niall. Save Dougal.

Cin could only do what he could do. He swept Jonathan into his arms and headed for the house. His mate was his first priority.

*

The universe zipped past Niall in a nauseating display. He half expected to be ripped to shreds at any moment. Pressure built inside his ears, making him wonder if his eardrums would explode. Air moved too fast to be taken into his lungs. Darkness crowded his vision. A second before it could take him under, his feet landed softly upon a solid white floor. In fact, everything was blindingly white. Niall fought the urge to shield his eyes.

Dark hair and emerald eyes captured his attention. Although they'd never met, Niall recognized Goddess Celeste immediately. His soul knew her. She was the creator of all vampire-kind. He fell to his knees and bowed his head

"Your excellency."

She snorted. "Is that what you're going with?"

He had no idea. Niall had never posed the philosophical question of how to refer to a god should they ever meet. "Ma'am?" he asked questioningly.

Goddess Celeste hummed. "It matters not. Do you think I make mistakes?"

Niall's voice came out stronger this time. "No."

She huffed. "For the love of all things holy, get off your knees. Maybe if you'd spent a little more time on them while you were alive, you wouldn't be in this mess."

His eyebrows shot to his hairline as he stood.

A rolled-up magazine appeared in her hand. She hit him with it. "Get your mind out of the gutter," she said, punctuating each word by hitting him with the magazine. "I meant on your knees in prayer." She turned slightly away before turning back again and meeting his gaze. Her eyes flashed with devilry. "Or did I?" She eyed him from head to toe and sighed. With the snap of her fingers, a chair appeared. "I've changed my mind. You're too tall to be hovering over me and giving me a crick in my neck."

Niall immediately sat.

She gave him a short nod as if satisfied by the difference in height now. "Let's start again. Do you think I make mistakes?"

"No," he repeated every bit as strong as he had the first time.

Celeste paced away. "Then why have you hurt your loves by fighting against them for so long? Have I not blessed you with more than others? Shown my favoritism?"

Niall's forehead furrowed in confusion.

"I'm sorry; I don't understand."

"Ah, so it's ignorance and not defiance." Her pacing slowed. While watching her feet, Celeste tapped the rolled-up magazine against her palm. "Perhaps a little blindness is also in this mix," she added, sounding thoughtful. She met his stare once more. "Do you love Cin?"

Niall dipped his chin. "I love all my men."

She hit him again. Her paper weapon caused more noise than pain, but her point was made. "Don't play dumb. That's unattractive, especially when speaking to someone who knows you better than you know yourself. Do you think I don't know how you've cared for him? How you've allowed your insecurities trick you into believing he loves you as he would any prince who rules him?"

Niall held his tongue. Anything he said

would only get him hit again.

"Damn right, it would," she spat, obviously reading his thoughts. "Gifts I've set at your feet for centuries have gone unnoticed, but this new perfection I've created for you cannot be ignored. It's too important," she said, sounding as if the last part was more for herself.

"I'm not ignoring Jonathan." As he said his mate's name, pain washed over him. Jonathan was on the verge of death, and he was stuck here. What would happen if he didn't make it back in time? Were they all already dead? A lump took up residence in his throat. Celeste paced as if oblivious to his inner turmoil.

"Jonathan," Celeste said lovingly. Indeed, her steps slowed as she stared off into space, smiling as she said his name— like she enjoyed the flavor of it on her tongue as much as Niall enjoyed having the man on his. "Is he not amazing?" she asked.

"He's dying," Niall growled, losing patience. "As we speak, he's bleeding to death with a gaping wound in his chest. I need to get back to him."

Goddess Celeste smiled as if pandering to a child. "I assure you, he's quite safe. My personal guard has been keeping close tabs on him and will ensure he is healed." Her gaze drifted away again, as if losing her train of thought. She smiled like a proud mother. "As long as Jonathan has been capable of speech, he's talked to me for countless hours—like a child who's eaten too much sugar. He rambles on about everything. Half the time, his thoughts aren't complete, but he never stops seeking answers from me." Her smile let Niall know this pleased her. "When he was twenty, I visited him in the night and set my hand upon him, giving him comfort when his grandmother passed. She'd been the only human who fully accepted him. That's my fault," Celeste said, her expression turning sad. "I gave him gifts, you see? Abilities usually reserved for the rarest of immortals. How could I not?" she asked, once more sounding as if she mused aloud. "You, my immortal soldiers, ignore my presence, while Jonathan, a man who was given nothing but a few short years on earth, speaks to me daily. You're spoiled."

Her hand shot out as if to strike Niall's cheek. At the last moment, she caressed him instead.

"As much as you think I don't understand your trials, you're wrong. I've existed since the dawn of all. No one knows better than me how cruel time is. He takes and takes, stealing everything until we are no more than shells." After taking a step back, her smile reappeared. "That's why Jonathan is so important.

That's why he's blessed." Celeste's smile slipped away. "That's why I gave him two warriors to worship him, and worship him, you shall. He's the key to everything." She moved closer, holding his stare with an intensity that held Niall in place with fear. "I'm about to show you the future, Niall, leader of the Hellish. You must keep it safe. You must keep Jonathan safe."

*

As Jonathan watched Faolan pace and Cin worry at his bottom lip, he tried to feel what they felt. He couldn't. Twice now he'd been the target of an attack. The last time, it had taken him weeks to shake the chill. Lire had done something to Jonathan, leaving him feeling euphoric and better than he had in ages. Cin had wasted no time rinsing the blood from Jonathan's chest, as if he needed to reassure himself Jonathan was okay. It had taken

Jonathan fifteen minutes of begging, telling Cin he loved him, and letting his mate feel his heartbeat before Cin allowed Jonathan to don a clean shirt.

Just when Jonathan thought Cin might snap under the strain, Faolan ended up being the one who broke.

"We should be out there, hunting the bastard who dared attack our prince." Faolan's face hardened. "We need to find that fooker who killed Dougal, rip off his demon head, and shit down his throat."

"We're not currently equipped to hunt Mammon, and that demon saved Jonathan," Cin said, sounding torn. "We need to find Niall."

The words Lire had whispered before disappearing rang in Jonathan's head. *I am Lire, seventh son of Asmodeus. Say my name and I will come to you.*

"Who is Asmodeus?"

Cin chewed on the side of his fingernail, looking ready to crawl out of his skin. "The seventh Prince of Hell—Lust. Why?"

Jonathan didn't respond. Cin's answer explained so much, especially why Lire was so powerful. "Niall is on his way, and Dougal isn't dead," Jonathan said instead, bringing two sets of eyes his way. Jonathan concentrated on the amethyst ones. The ones that held the most pain. "He isn't dead."

In two long strides, Faolan reached his side. After falling to his knees, Faolan's gaze met Jonathan's. Hope and desperation swirled in the man's mind. "How do you know? The demon said a life for a life."

Jonathan's hand moved without

thought. Faolan reached for him at the same time, as if needing comfort only Jonathan could give. A smile pulled at the corners of Jonathan's mouth. He could feel Lire and Dougal getting farther away. All the way to the Port of Southern Louisiana, to be exact. "Because I can feel him," Jonathan said, doing a piss-poor job of explaining himself. "I can feel all of you. Them too. I can feel everyone."

Faolan shook his head. "What did that demon do to you? Are you high?"

Jonathan shook his head. "I've always known all of you were there. My whole life, I've been searching for you. I just didn't understand what I was looking for."

"Us," Niall said, strolling into the room as if he hadn't been sent God only knows where. "You were searching for us." He tossed boxes of chalk to Faolan and Cin. "Ward the walls. Start with this room.

While you draw the protection spells, I'll talk," Niall said before leaning down and capturing Jonathan's mouth.

"Where the hell have you been?" Faolan snapped.

Niall didn't break their kiss.

A flavor like cotton candy ice cream coated Jonathan's taste buds. He held tight to Niall's shirt, incapable of letting him go. Evil was always trying to tear them apart. The fear he'd been stamping down flared to life.

"You smell like a candy store," Jonathan whispered against Niall's lips to hold the panic at bay.

"I love you, baby. Please stop scaring me. I'm an old man. It's not good for my heart."

Cin appeared over his shoulder. "Yes.

Please stop doing that."

"And you," Niall said, snagging Cin's hand and pulling him in the center of things. "I love you too. You two are my world. We all have way too much to lose to be so careless with our lives." Without giving anyone time to respond, Niall kissed Cin. Tears welled in Jonathan's eyes. He hadn't believed they'd find their way. Before he could coo over it—the way he wanted—Niall pulled him into their kiss.

"For fook's sake. I'm like the fourth wheel over here and that doesn't even make sense," Faolan said, making Jonathan laugh.

Niall smacked Cin's ass. "Get back to work. We have to fortify this place until we can come up with a solid plan to battle Mammon. Two attacks on Jonathan isn't a coincidence, and this is a whole new level of problems."

"They know he's our weakness," Cin said as he moved to the closest wall and drew a circle.

Niall shook his head. "They know he's our greatest strength, and they won't stop until he's destroyed." All heads swiveled in Niall's direction. "I didn't capture that demon by some stroke of luck. He let me catch him. And that was no ordinary demon."

Jonathan had known that last part, but not the first. "Why would he do that?" Jonathan didn't understand. Why would anyone subject himself to torture unnecessarily?

"Because Goddess Celeste asked it of him."

Faolan's mouth fell open.

Cin visibly floundered. "What? How? Why?"

"Who is Goddess Celeste?"

Niall smiled at Jonathan's question. "Your greatest ally. In your life, you've known her as God, and she thinks the world of you."

"I don't understand." Jonathan couldn't stop playing ignorant because he was.

Cin waved his arms wildly. "How do you know how she feels about Jonathan?"

"Because she told me," Niall said, sounding proud. "That's where I've been."

Cin looked as if he'd been shocked speechless. Faolan didn't suffer any such ailment. "Is it because Jonathan is a Seer, and what about Dougal? Was he there? Jonathan says he's still alive."

"Dougal is fine. He'll find his way back to us. If not, Jonathan can find him any time he likes. Right, Jonathan?"

Jonathan swallowed. He didn't know why it was true, but it was. "Yes."

"You're not a Seer," Niall said while holding Jonathan's gaze. "You never were."

Jonathan found himself leaning forward in his seat, hanging on Niall's every word. "I don't understand," he repeated, because he couldn't stop.

"If he's not a Seer, then what? He's never been full human. The boy knows too many things," Faolan argued.

"I know he does," Niall said, holding Jonathan's stare. "That's because he's a Nephilim. Goddess Celeste's great-grandson, to be precise."

Holy shit. Jonathan didn't even know where to start. All he knew for certain was, he had the best clan to keep him safe while they figured this out.

Keep an eye out for Book Three, Crave.

ABOUT THE AUTHOR

Charity Parkerson is an award winning and multi-published author with several companies. Born with no filter from her brain to her mouth, she decided to take this odd quirk and insert it in her characters.

*2015 Readers' Favorite Award Winner
*Winner of 2, 2014 Readers' Favorite Awards
*2015 Passionate Plume Award Finalist
*2013 Readers' Favorite Award Winner
*2013 Reviewers' Choice Award Winner
*2012 ARRA Finalist for Favorite Paranormal Romance
*Five-time winner of The Mistress of the Darkpath

Connect with her online:

--Join my street team: facebook.com/TeamCharityParkerson
--Sign up for my newsletter: http://bit.ly/CharityNews
--Website: charityparkerson.com
--Facebook: facebook.com/authorCharityParkerson
facebook.com/TheMenofSin
--Twitter: twitter.com/CharityParkerso